MW00758276

AMERICAN HEROES PRESS

SHORT STORY ANTHOLOGY

WHAT IS A HERO?

American Heroes Press
1663 Liberty Drive, Suite 200
Bloomington, IN 47403

First published by American Heroes Press on 7/29/2009.

Printed in the United States of America.
This book is printed on acid-free paper.

TABLE OF CONTENTS

Foreword
by American Heroes Press Founder, Lieutenant
Raymond E. Foster, LAPD (ret.)   vii

Tun Tavern Fraternity
By James Drew Pointkouski (Grand Prize Winner) 1

The Legend of Robert "Sweet Bobby" Moore
By James H. Lilley (First Runner-Up)   21

The Day Cambria Got Buzzed
By Steve Gilmore (Second Runner-Up)   43

My Brother, My Hero
By Mark Lambert (Finalist)   61

My Hero Jim
By Jody Lilley (Finalist)   67

Aldo and the Giant
By Mike Stamm (Finalist)   73

The Christmas Carol Project
By Mike Stamm (Finalist)   85

Freak of Nature
By Mike Stamm (Finalist)   99

My American Heroes: The warriors of HMLS
302
By Robert P. Mueck (Finalist)   115

Behind the Badge
By Susan Tutko   125

Dangers, Toils, and Snares
By Tim Casey   138

Leonard C. Kasson
By Wayne E. Beyea   147

A Day Off From the Farm: A U.S. Marine in
Vietnam
By Zach Foster   155

FOREWORD

by American Heroes Press Founder, Lieutenant Raymond E. Foster, LAPD (ret.)

What is a Hero?

This collection of short stories indirectly asks the question - what is a hero? Each of the 13 authors wrote about a specific person whom the author identified as an American Hero. Each author had a different take - some heroes were thrust into danger; others were comedic, yet heroic; still others were role models because of their heroic nature. While all different, there is a common thread: heroism.

What makes a person heroic is the conscious decision to place the needs of others before the needs of self. It is not danger that makes a person heroic. Danger is a situation and although people can act heroically when faced with danger, it's the person, not the situation that is heroic. When a firefighter rescues someone from a burning building, a police officer confronts an armed suspect or a soldier pulls a wounded comrade from the line of fire, the essential and common thread is the hero placed the needs of someone else above their own. Selflessness under fire magnifies that existing heroic nature of the individual.

I think that all the definitions of hero have it wrong. It's not showing courage; great ability; great achievements; or being a warrior. It is putting someone else first. This may be why we see so many people at the pinnacle of success thanking their parents; or, why so many people identify their own parents as heroes. Because we recognize that parents are heroes because they put their children's needs before their own. Indeed, while these stories focus on military, fire and police, they could have easily focused on teachers, parents or volunteers.

Some of these stories are about Valor; that is, courage in the face of danger. More commonly, the heroic nature is the subtle "others first" theme. What I hope you find in the stories is that you too, are an American Hero. While you may never drag someone from a burning car, there are plenty of opportunities to be heroic by putting others first.

Lieutenant Raymond E. Foster, LAPD (ret.)

Tun Tavern Fraternity

By James Drew Pointkouski
(Grand Prize Winner)

Philadelphia, Pennsylvania – "Birthplace of Freedom"

Late 1979 – Early 1980

The 70's were almost gone; the dawn of a new decade was fast approaching. Democratic President Jimmy Carter had left his mark on Philadelphia in the form of high gas prices and even higher property taxes. At 20 years old, I felt incubated against the harsh world all around me. As a college student, I still didn't know what I wanted to be when I grew up. Little did I know, but this was all about to change just like the decade.

Early on the night of November 4, 1979 I was watching television, snuggled with my girlfriend Barbie Avalon in her parent's row home in South Philadelphia. We had grown close since meeting about a year prior. Her mother really liked me too and never missed an opportunity to bring up the subject of marriage. Her sister,

Wendy could pass for an international model or perhaps an Italian film star. Wendy never missed an opportunity to flirt with me just to goad her sister. Barbie had all the looks of Wendy without the stuck-up attitude possessed by the elder sibling. Whenever I visited their home, these three women seemed to care for my every need, going out of their way to wait on me hand and foot. Needless to say, I really enjoyed my time at the Avalon home!

Then there was Barbie's father Anthony, a second generation Italian-American who averaged eighty hours a week running his own construction company. He was your typical blue-collar, hard working, family man that made this country so great. Yet he seemed to despise me with every hard working bone in his body to the core of his being. To him, I was an outsider – I wasn't Italian, I didn't live in South Philly and I didn't work with my hands. I was a college boy, he didn't like me and I just was not right for his precious daughter. What made matters worse; he saw how "his baby" looked at me. He also saw how his older daughter treated me. And still worse, his wife did nothing but constantly sing my praises. Every time I came around, Mr. Avalon would eye me with utter disgust then suddenly smile an evil grin. I figured that one day I would end up in a cement grave under one of his construction sites. Today, however, I was seated on his sofa, safely entwined in the arms of his youngest daughter.

The television program we were watching was interrupted by a newsflash: "The American Embassy in

Iran was overtaken today by rebellious university students, who stormed the embassy gates and eventually took the entire American contingent hostage." I barely knew where Iran was located but I had a sudden thought: "If the US was going to war, I had better start preparing." I knew in my heart America would not stand for this transgression – even that liberal, peanut farming president could not stand by and let this happen. So, on this cold November evening, I knew I had to do something; I knew I must enlist. Barbie would never understand but maybe now I would be able to escape whatever evil plan her father had devised for me.

I kept a daily watch on this tragic news story and decided I would enter the Armed Forces before the upcoming war broke out - I wanted to be fully prepared. A few short weeks later, I marched my young patriotic ass into the local United States Marine Corps recruiting office. When I entered the recruiting facility, the tightly muscled, iron-jawed Gunnery Sergeant behind the desk eyed me with suspicion. He asked briefly why I wanted to join the Marines over all the other services and about my background. An eyebrow rose upon his leathery features, and he seemed surprised that I had a couple years of college. Almost like a salesman, he asked me to take a short quiz right then and there. He explained that the quiz would help him to ascertain my basic proficiency and would accurately gauge my performance on the full military ASVAB entrance test.

Gunny sat me at the desk adjacent to his own and gave me a small blue test booklet. A short while after completing the quiz, I double checked my work and returned the paperwork to the Gunny. While he graded my test, I looked around the office at various Marine Corps paraphernalia and admired the recruiter's crisp uniform. The creases on both his khaki shirt and blue trousers looked like they could cut you. A few moments later, the recruiter startled me as he loudly exclaimed, "No shit! Hey kid, you aced the test. You are eligible for any MOS in the Corps!" At this point, the Gunnery Sergeant seemed a bit more earnest and we spoke at length about life and training in the Corps. I remember walking out of the office, not only was I excited but it felt like a great weight was lifted off my shoulders – I now knew my future: I would be one of the Few, the Proud, the Marines.

A couple days later I took the complete, long version of the military ASVAB entrance test at the military testing center in downtown Philadelphia. Early that morning, Gunny Iron-jaw himself, picked me up at my home in a grey colored U. S. Government sedan. We drove directly to the Cherry Street office building amid morning chaos in Philadelphia that is wrongly named 'rush hour.' As we sat in the heavy traffic along Interstate 95, I recall thinking that I had never seen such a grey day – grey sky, grey car, grey clouds, grey city – little did I know all this grey was a good omen! Later in a large room filled with rows of desks, myself and about forty other military candidates from throughout Philly, were seated alphabetically and spaced out, seated in every other chair. Without much pretense, the exam was administered under the watchful eyes of a Marine Corps Master Sergeant. After completing the test, Gunny Iron-jaw whispered that he wanted to introduce me to someone. He took me down a back hallway to a small basement office, where I met a nattily dressed man by the name of Mr. Grey.

MR. GREY – "A Silver Lining?"

Deep within the bowels of the testing center sat a small room which, appropriately, was painted industrial grey. It was furnished simply: a small metal desk sat against the side wall with a swivel chair behind it, a standard metal folding chair sat in front of it, angled to one side. There was a small desk lamp and centered in front of the lamp was a plain manila folder. What immediately caught my eye was that the folder was imprinted with my name and social security number. I entered the small office, as Gunny quietly introduced me to Mr. Grey, who immediately arose from behind the desk and extended a firm handshake. He was about 6 foot even and approximately 185 lbs but he had a grip like an iron vise. When he smiled –I had never seen teeth or the collar of a shirt so white – they seemed to glow in the dimly lit room, a stark contrast to the grey all around. Mr. Grey gestured for me to sit in the folding chair. While he took his seat, Grey removed his tweed sports jacket and hung it on the chair back. This action revealed that Grey wore a handgun in a leather holster on his right hip. I thought perhaps he was a police detective. My mind did a quick inventory of all my youthful escapades and could not think of any reason to fear arrest - so I wondered what all this was about?

As Grey began to speak he paused, looked into the manila folder then directly in my eyes and asked, "Why do you want to be a Marine?" I explained to him my entire thought process since seeing the American Embassy in Tehran on the news flash. Grey listened intently while I rambled on, and then asked, "So you want to serve your country?" I answered, "Yes sir, and I want to be one of the best!" Afterward, we spoke briefly about my family and my reasons for leaving college to enlist.

At this point, I believed that Grey was probably a Marine Officer – thinking that's why he was interested in my education. But then he said, "What I want you to do Pointkouski is report to Boot Camp in Parris Island and do your absolute best. Upon graduation, we will talk some more – hows that sound?" "Good, sir" was all I could reply. As we left the small office, Gunny led me back to join the other candidates. I sat there wondering, "What in the hell was that all about?" I never worked up the nerve to ask Gunny anything further about this cryptic meeting. Instead, I theorized that they were interested in me becoming an officer but were probably concerned by the fact that I had not yet finished my degree. They would first make sure I proved myself in

Boot Camp! Shortly thereafter, raising my right hand, I swore "to defend my country against all enemies, foreign and domestic." Reality set in - I just joined the Marine Corps!

Parris Island, South Carolina - "We Don't Promise You a Rose Garden"
September 1980 – December 1980

For those of you who are reading this today, I'm sure you have seen movies like "Full Metal Jacket," so I won't bore you with all the particulars of arriving at Marine Corps Recruit Depot. In the muggy Carolina darkness, I stood at attention on yellow painted footprints thinking, "What have I got myself into?" Thus began 12 weeks of pure torture, mental and physical anguish, deep soul searching and hard core, elite military training. I loved every second of it! Never before had I felt so alive. Never had I felt so purposeful. In the middle of this hot autumn South Carolina night, I was received into boot camp to the sounds of yelling and screaming. "Welcome to MCRD Parris Island – the first and last words out of your filthy sewers will be Sir. Do you understand me Recruits?" "Yes Sir."

Four men – not mere mortals but military demigods were to guide me to hell and back: Senior Drill Instructor Gunnery Sergeant Bjelko, and his cadre of Drill Instructors, Staff Sergeant Britton, Staff Sergeant Caldwell, and Sergeant Williams. These men ran my new world. I could write an entire book about Boot Camp alone, so I'll save the details for another time. Suffice it to say, I forgot all about Mr. Grey during these 12 weeks and focused totally on my new role as a Marine recruit.

As the song goes, *"I was born on Parris Island, the land that God forgot, where the sand is eighteen inches deep, and the sun is blazing hot!"* I discovered a lot about myself there. I also learned a new skill that would redefine my life. One which I was never previously exposed … rifle marksmanship! *"This is my rifle, there are many like it but this one is mine …"* so goes the creed. We learned to shoot the "Marine Corps Way" – the most effective marksmanship training program in the world. This training is taken very seriously because their motto is "every Marine, a rifleman." No matter what their MOS, every Marine must master firearms training. It's part of their warrior way, their Marine ethos! For me, I would not settle on merely qualifying as a Marksman or Sharpshooter – I sought to be an Expert!

Twelve weeks on the "Island" take an eternity. You are fully immersed in their world, playing by their rules and know nothing of the outside world. Marine Drill Instructors are damn effective. Slowly they mold a group of individual civilians, forged together through the crucible of pain and sweat, into highly efficient, basically trained Marines. During training, we were constantly reminded that we trained for war.

I graduated Boot Camp in December of 1980 – a fit young stud in a crisp Dress Blue uniform. Adorned with "mosquito wings," the single chevron of a meritoriously promoted Private First Class, I also wore the coveted "crossed rifles badge" of an expert rifleman. So full of pride that my heart threatened to rip right through the Blue coat. There were tears in my eyes and a lump in my throat as I thanked my DI's for the last time and bid farewell to my mates. Then, we all departed Parris Island on a short Christmas home leave. Soon, my new "band of brothers" would all report to new duty stations throughout the Fleet Marine Force for more advanced training. The Marine Corps has two missions: The first is to train Marines and the second is to fight wars. With training almost complete, I now wanted to go to war. Little did I know I would soon get my wish.

Philadelphia, PA - "You Can Never Go Back"
December 1980 - January 1981

Philly, by the way, is also the birthplace of the Marine Corps. On November 10, 1775 Marines began life in a little pub called *Tun Tavern* located in Colonial Philadelphia. The exact site now sits below modern day Interstate 95. You've got to love an Armed Force that was founded in a bar … just picture this scene: over a few pints of ale, "Alright lads, this is what we're gonna do: We'll go out aboard Navy ships, come alongside the enemy vessels, swing aboard on ropes, then we'll destroy everything and everyone in sight! Now who's in?"... At first it felt nice to be home from Boot Camp – back in Philly, the City of Brotherly Love and home of cheese steaks and soft pretzels. Proud to be from the same birthplace as the Corps!

Meanwhile, in my parent's home, it was a different story. While I was gone, my basement bedroom had been removed and the room was remodeled into a recreation room. I guess it's true, once you leave home, there's no going back! It felt so claustrophobic there that I actually missed the "Island." As quickly as I could get out the door, I sought the relief of seeing my friends. My friends were all very interested in hearing about boot camp but something was "strange" there too! Everyone just seemed … well, the same and I felt so different. As we talked, I still felt very close but I surmised we were suddenly growing in different directions. Unbeknownst to me, all the Marines from recruit platoon 2087 were experiencing similar feelings at this same time. Once a Marine, Always a Marine – we are forever changed to the core of our beings.

That night I met up with my friends who decided to throw me an impromptu welcome home party. *General Grant's Saloon* – a popular watering hole at the intersection of Grant Avenue and Roosevelt Boulevard was our favorite spot, chosen for its good food and inexpensive pitchers of beer. After the party had been in full swing for a couple hours, I needed to relieve my near bursting bladder. Having consumed too many ice cold beers, I stumbled toward the restroom, which to my friend's amusement I now called the 'head.' The men's room was located next to the kitchen, midway between the bar and the dinning area. The pit stop brought sweet relief. Then while at the sink, an unassuming man, wearing a leather flight jacket, entered the small restroom. He pushed open all the stall doors then said, "Hey congratulations Marine." I responded, "Thank you, sir" as I dried my hands with some paper C-fold towels. The man seemed satisfied no one else was in the small restroom, and before I could reach the door, Mr. Flight Jacket said, "We have a mutual friend … Mr. Grey would like you to call him tomorrow morning at 8:00 AM." He handed me a small index card printed with a seven digit number. Before I could respond, he said, "Good luck, kid" and was gone out of the bathroom door where he disappeared into the crowed bar.

The encounter seemed to sober me – I looked at my reflection in the bathroom mirror, splashed some water on my face and mouthed to myself, "What the hell?" Suddenly, my buddy Tom came crashing through the restroom door screaming/slurring, "Watdafuckcha do, fall in?" I laughed and punched him in the arm as we passed. Shouting back over my shoulder I gibed, "If you shake that thing more than twice, you're playing with it!" I walked out to the sound of Tom "saying a short prayer to the porcelain gods" as he puked into the urinal. I quickly scanned the interior of the bar and then looked out into the parking lot. No flight jacket anywhere in sight; He was gone. I paused a few moments before going back into the bar. The temperature had dropped considerably since my arrival but the crisp cold air felt good in my lungs compared to the smoky interior of the bar. Finally, I walked inside *Grants* to rejoin my friends and jammed the phone number into my pocket.

I sat back down at our table and took a sip of beer but my mind was no longer into the party. I kept thinking about what just transpired and what that would mean in my life. Would I have to go back to school to enter an Officer Training Program? I'd forgotten all about Mr. Grey. I was just getting into my new enlisted Marine role – would I now have to change everything and start over again? My mind was racing. Feeling a soft hand on my neck brought me back to the present. My girlfriend had just arrived at *Grant's*; she had been working late at a second job to get some extra cash for Christmas. "Shit, Christmas – I have to go shopping for gifts!" I thought. Suddenly, she gave me a big wet kiss to a chorus of drunken "woo hoo's" and "get a room" called out from the crowd. Barbie had been mad at me for joining the Marines and I wasn't sure if she were coming tonight. Hell, I wasn't sure until now that she ever wanted to see me again. I took the cue from the crowd and whispered for her to drive me home. I had to get out of there.

After making my way around the table of friends for what seemed like a hundred drunken hugs and good byes later, Barbie & I exited the pub arm-in-arm. An anonymous patron seated at the bar yelled out, "Semper

Fi Marine! Go storm her beachhead!" which made us laugh out loud. In that playful moment, Barbie and I grabbed each other and kissed soulfully while looking deeply into each other's eyes. I knew right then she really loved me. Unfortunately for her, I also knew at that very moment we would never live the life together she dreamed about. The short ride home was uncomfortably quiet. She looked hurt and genuinely surprised that I wanted to go directly inside without any "extra curricular activities." I gave her a quick peck and promised to call. As I thanked her for the ride, I reassured her that I was just extremely tired. That night, I could barely sleep as my mind continued to think about the unknown. It probably didn't help that I now had to crash on the living room sofa. Maybe I should have gone home with Barbie to her new apartment. I could have cut a quick slice and snuggled up with her to sleep comfortably in a real bed. Well, that's a big maybe! "Who the hell is this Mr. Grey anyway?"

Morning, December 23, 1980

Despite my dreadful sleep, I woke up around 6:30 AM alert, refreshed and hangover-free. Like boot camp, I began to tighten the sheets, and then realized I was home. So I just stripped the linens from the couch, changed into PT gear (sweats and running shoes) and joined my mother in the kitchen. She had already made coffee and it smelled incredible. I grabbed a hot mug and sat at the kitchen table with her, where she perused the Philadelphia Inquirer. I tried to read the sports page to catch up on the Eagles, who were making a run for the Super Bowl. Mom peered at me over the top of her coffee cup – I felt it before actually seeing her look at me. She seemed apprehensive. I asked, "What's up mom?" She hesitated, and then blurted out, "You know, if you really don't want to do this I can give you a little money to go to Canada or something!" I was stunned as if I were just hit between the eyes with a boot camp pugil stick. I didn't know how to respond. I didn't know what to say. I was confused; angry that she didn't get me. After another swallow of steaming java, I finally said, "Mom, I know you don't understand but I love what I am doing – I chose to enlist and I'm doing well." Tears welled up in her eyes. Great, that's two women I've disappointed in just a few hours. I knew any further conversation was pointless, so I went outside for my morning run.

The chill of this late December morning snapped my mind back to attention and my body quickly followed. Nothing better than a nice five mile run to clear the head and sharpen the senses! Immediately I fell into a Marine Corps rhythmic gait. Cadence calls from the Island rang in my head; I set about a seven minute per mile pace. Common scenes of my neighborhood passed by with each step, evoking many youthful memories which soon were replaced by recent scenes and recollections of boot camp: P.T., the obstacle course, the confidence course, the parade deck, Bowman's Beach, the rifle range … *"my rifle and I are deadly, one shot, one kill!"*

Left, right, left …."Lo, right a lo, right a, lo right ley 'eft, lefty right ley 'eft, lo right ley 'eft, lefty double time …" The cadence set the pace, it controlled my breathing; the run was effortless! Afterward, I felt renewed – body, mind and spirit. Before going back inside, I lingered a few minutes and watched as the neighborhood began to come to life. People rushing from their home to their cars – cursing under their breath at the cold, while they scraped the frost from the windshields. It's like I was invisible – no one even noticed me standing there. Everyone too preoccupied in their own little world.

After a quick shower and some fresh clothes, I entered the living room and checked the time on the grandfather clock. One of my father's prized possessions, he is meticulous with its care and the time is always correct. 7:55 AM; I dug out the buck slip from the pocket of last night's jeans and sat next to the hall telephone. 8:00 AM sharp, I picked up the receiver and dialed the digits 346-2250 with a good amount of expectation; yet I knew not what to expect.

Second ring, "Good Morning, Tun Tavern" said the sexiest female voice you've ever heard. "What the hell," I thought but said, "PFC Pointkouski calling for Mr. Grey." "One moment please, he's expecting your call!" was her sweet reply. Almost instantly … "Hello Drew, glad you are punctual – a good trait to have! How was your run?" "How the hell? ..." but Mr. Grey cut me off as he continued, "PT is good for your body, mind and soul. But enough small talk, in fifteen minutes, a driver will be by to pick you up. Throw on your Winter Service "A" uniform and tell your parents you are helping the Marine Recruiter today, got it?" I began to respond with a, "yes sir" but the connection was broken before I could form the words. I thought aloud, "I'm glad Grey was expecting my call – I can't imagine if he were rushed."

At precisely 8:15 AM, a black sedan pulled in front of my parent's home and honked the horn twice. I had just put a final buff on my spit shined shoes using a piece of nylon stocking – a trick shared with us by Sgt. Williams before our final inspection on Parris Island. I quickly yelled good bye to my parents and bounded out the front door taking the stairs two at a time, slipped on an icy patch, recovered and then ran down the driveway toward the waiting vehicle. The driver was none other than Mr. Flight Jacket. As I approached the car, he motioned for me to get into the rear passenger side door, which I did. I said, "Good morning sir. Where are we going?" His reply was a bit gruff, "We're going where I take you. And you are to sit in the back and shut the fuck up. Got it?" I got it alright – the one thing you can bet money on – a young Marine can definitely follow orders! I sat back and kept my mouth shut the entire ride but still wondered to myself where we were heading.

The sedan sped through the blue collar neighborhood, turned right onto Knights Road, another right onto

Frankford Avenue and proceeded southward for several lights. We passed Linden Avenue and then finally made a left onto the access to Interstate 95, then continued southbound on I-95. Soon we exited at the Cottman Avenue ramp and approached the old Frankford Arsenal complex on State Road. Mr. Flight Jacket flashed some credentials to the uniformed guard who lifted a barrier gate for us to pass. We wove through the complex of brick buildings and parked next to a dumpster behind one of the buildings. It was more of an alleyway than a driveway but it abutted a high chain link fence which was topped with razor wire. There was a second fence which paralleled the first, leaving about thirty feet between them, with nothing but woods beyond the fences. The driver directed me to enter the building through the unmarked steel door at the rear of the building. I finally spoke to thank Mr. Flight Jacket and he barked, "Don't thank me son – I get thanked twice a month on payday." He advised his name was Mr. White and told me he would be driving me home later in the day. Stepping out of the car, I straightened my gig line, took a deep breath and entered the building.

Inside the sleek foyer, I approached a beautiful blonde seated at the receptionist desk. Before I could speak, she said, "Good morning PFC, welcome to Tun Tavern. Mr. Grey will be right with you," as she motioned to a leather sofa along the opposite wall. On the granite wall above the sofa was a small brass plaque that read, "Tun Tavern, established 1775." A few moments later, an equally gorgeous brunette stepped from the only visible interior door and said, "Mr. Grey will see you now."

Mr. Grey's office was ten times as large as my parent's entire living room. Furthermore, it was furnished a hell of a lot nicer than the tiny little closet of an office where we first met on Cherry Street. Grey sprung out of his desk chair, met me midway in the center of a plush Afghan carpet and greeted me with another one of his vise-like handshakes. Even though I am about two inches taller and twenty pounds heavier than Mr. Grey, I felt small in his presence. He was dressed in a dark Navy blue single breasted suit and black wing-tipped shoes which caught my eye because their shine rivaled my own spit-shined duty oxfords. Instead of gesturing me toward a seat, he motioned for me to follow him to the side wall which was covered entirely with a map of the world. Closer examination revealed that there were little colored stick pins stuck into the map at various locations. Above the map were a row of clocks which were set for different times according to the world zone. There was one each for Washington D.C., Rio de Janeiro, London, Rome, Frankfurt, Moscow, Tehran, Calcutta, Beijing, and Tokyo, which were labeled on small brass plates.

Grey turned to me and said, "Today, we continue the tradition which began long ago by men just like ourselves – to the Corps." My mind really racing now, I had to ask, "Sir, are you a Marine?" His reply came with a smile. "Of course … well, technically yes and no. You know the saying, 'Once a Marine, Always a Marine' right

Drew? You still don't get it yet do you? I thought you said you wanted to serve your country?" he said accusingly. I blurted, "I do, and that's why I joined the Marines!" Grey put his arm around my shoulders and gestured once again toward the map. The world is a dangerous place. We have an excellent new President right now in Ronald Reagan. I briefed him just last month about our entire program and he is - how shall I say? - *Very enthusiastic* about our unit. I spoke to him about you too – as our newest member. The President asked about your training timetable and told me to bring you to meet him. We have an appointment for next Friday morning." "What?" I asked, almost blubbering. Grey raised his tone, "Son, we ARE going to D.C. next Friday to chat with the Boss, got it?" "Sir, Yes Sir!" "Welcome to Tun Tavern Fraternity – we serve at the sole discretion of the Commander-in-Chief, the President of the United States of America!" Have a seat son, I'll tell you all about our fraternity.

The End.

Tun Tavern Fraternity

About the Author

J. Drew Pointkouski is a Marine Corps Veteran who served in the 2nd Marine Division and on embassy duty with the elite Marine Security Guard Battalion in Reykjavik, Iceland and La Paz, Bolivia. After being honorably discharged, he completed undergraduate studies and began his current career in law enforcement.

He resides in Central New Jersey with his wife, Alleah and their four children. Presently pursuing a post-graduate degree, Drew is a part-time author and life member of the Marine Corps League, where he writes for his detachment newsletter and veterans history project.

THE LEGEND OF ROBERT "SWEET BOBBY" MOORE

By James H. Lilley
(First Runner-Up)

Robert W. Moore, a man known by such nicknames as "Sweet Bobby, The Animal, The Lizard and Sweetness," is a former Marine, Baltimore City, and Howard County, Maryland Police Officer. Oftentimes it is difficult to find just the right words to describe Bob. A human being who seemed impervious to pain, and a man described by many to possess the strength of a Grizzly Bear. Bob is a man that, if for some reason during a moment of complete insanity, you harbored a notion that you'd like to try and kick his ass, you'd better do so from behind. Of course, if you were overcome by that thought, you should be armed with a sledgehammer or a tractor-trailer, and pray to God that your assault didn't simply piss him off.

Sweetness was known far and wide for a most notorious trademark—his laugh. A laugh that seemed to rise up from within the depths of his being. A very deep "heh, heh, heh." And, that "heh, heh, heh" always seemed to come out of him at the most peculiar times—like when someone pulled a gun on him, or threatened to kick his ass.

Stories surrounding Bob's exploits were told over and over in restaurants, bars, around dinner tables, in homes and on street corners. Some listened in awe, while others didn't believe the fables, but those who knew the truth, admired Bob's bravado and held him near and dear in their hearts. Police officers under his command were comfortable knowing he would stand by them in good times and bad. And, police officers facing danger always prayed that he would be nearby, or on the way to help them. As for me, I'm happy and proud to say I've called Bob my friend for over 40 years.

The tales of Robert "The Animal" Moore are from another era. Restless times of race riots, flag and draft card burning. A time when young men marched off to war in a place called Vietnam, and came home to jeers instead of a hero's welcome. Indeed, it was a time when the legend of "Sweet Bobby" grew to be as real as the morning sunrise.

Motor Vehicle Matrimony

The County Seat of Howard County, Ellicott City, long held a reputation as *the* place where you could just drop by any time, day or night, and get married. People would travel from New York and even Florida in search of a Justice of the Peace, or minister to join them in wedlock. Yet, much to their dismay, those giddy travelers soon found Ellicott City's renown to be nothing more than a myth.

It was an unusually boring Friday evening and Bob was assigned the task of Night Shift Duty Officer. He had just settled down behind the desk to look over a stack of paperwork when a taxicab stopped in front of the police station. After a few minutes, a couple stumbled from the backseat and staggered, arm in arm, toward the front door of the building. Somehow they managed to make it to the desk, where they announced very loudly to Bob, "We're in love and wanna get married."

Suddenly the lobby was filled with coughs, guffaws, chokes and a round of not so discreet comments. "Man, you've gotta be kidding. She's so ugly she has to back up to a glass of water to get a drink," one of the officers said.

She giggled, and the man explained that he had been at sea for months as a Merchant Marine. Soon after returning to port he collected his pay, which was rather substantial, and set out to quench his thirst. He located a "respectable" establishment on Baltimore's world famous Block, and began to wash away all those months of loneliness. Somewhere between his first drink and mild intoxication, the woman of his dreams came in and sat down beside him. "It was love at first sight," he said to

Bob. After several rounds of drinks to celebrate finding true love, they decided to marry.

"Jesus, she's so ugly she'd make a train take a dirt road," someone said from behind him. "You can't be serious about marrying her."

He attempted to stand up straight. "I'm in love with this woman and I wanna marry her."

Bob leaned back in his chair, nodded and smiled. "Look, why don't you just go to a motel and spend the night? Get to know each other a little better, if you know what I mean? If you're still in love in the morning, then make arrangements to get married." The man shook his head. "No. I wanna do the right thing. I don't wanna make love to this woman until we're man and wife."

Bob explained that they could no longer drive to Ellicott City and get married on the spur of the moment. They hung their heads, and seemed on the verge of tears when a very mischievous twinkle appeared in Bob's eyes. "I can help you, though."

"Really," the man said. "How?"

"I have the authority to perform a temporary marriage ceremony." A few officers scurried laughing into a nearby men's room. "But, you've gotta remember this is only a temporary marriage. It's good only until eight o'clock Monday morning. After that, if you decide that you still wanna be married, you'll hafta apply for a license, find a minister and have another ceremony."

Of course, the loving couple was elated and agreed to be temporarily joined in wedded bliss. Bob opened the restroom door and summoned two officers to stand as witnesses while he joined the happy couple in holy matrimony. With witnesses holding their breath beside the blushing couple, Bob reached into the desk and pulled out a copy of the Maryland Motor Vehicle Code. Adjusting his ascot, and with a rather official flair, he opened the book, appropriately it seemed, to the section prohibiting reckless driving.

In a world record ceremony, Bob pronounced them man and wife, but would take one last step to make everything seem more official. He called Officer Wayne Ridgely to the station and told him to give the newly weds a police escort to a motel. Wayne grinned, and a moment later with lights flashing and siren wailing he escorted the taxicab to Brown's Motel on U. S. Route 40.

When the siren faded in the distance, Bob sat down. "Heh, heh, heh. When that guy wakes up in the morning, it's gonna be bad enough that he'll probably have the worst hangover in his entire life. But, when he rolls over and sees his bride, I bet he'll run all the way to the bay bridge and jump off the top span."

The Howard Place Chainsaw Massacre

The Howard Place was a local hangout noted for its good food, cold drinks, and live entertainment. The clientele was a mix of varying backgrounds from lawyers, police officers, and college students to construction workers. Everybody got along well and enjoyed sitting around the bar or tables talking, sharing a drink, listening to music and dancing.

"Sweet Bobby" was a regular visitor to the Howard Place, and usually stopped by for a steak and a cold drink. Mind you, Bob was very particular in the way he wanted his steak prepared. "I want a steak, very, very tender and very, very rare. Have the steer walk by the fire and cut off a slice." And, he meant every word of it.

One evening, after a long day of cutting down trees and stacking firewood, Bob stopped by for a steak dinner. There was an unusually large crowd there for a weekday, but the band playing that evening had a huge following. Bob sat down at the bar beside Officer Robert Reid, and gave his order to the bartender. He looked over at Reid after placing his order and said, "I probably should've just ordered the whole steer. I really worked up an appetite out there today."

Ronnie Jones, the owner of the Howard Place, was seated to Bob's right and was there when the dinner order arrived. Within a matter of seconds "Sweetness" complained to him that the steak was very tough. Jones, of course, disagreed, saying it was merely Bob's overactive imagination.

"Hell, I couldn't cut this thing with my chainsaw."

Reid wouldn't dare let the moment pass. "Moore, you ain't got a hair on your ass if you don't get your chainsaw and prove it."

Bob left the bar as the band began its second set of the evening. Moments later he returned to the bar carrying a large chainsaw. Certainly nobody believed the grinning, man-bear holding the saw would really fire it up and cut the steak. They stared in disbelief as he cranked up the saw and began attacking the steak. Smoke belched out and began filling the restaurant and bar. Soon, French-fries, lettuce, tomato and steak were flying around the bar. The band stopped playing, and the crowd started to laugh and cheer Bob on as he continued his assault on the steak.

"Christ, Bob, shut it off. I'll get you another steak," Ronnie Jones screamed over the roar of the chainsaw.

Bob stopped the saw, put it against the wall and sat down. He glanced over at Reid. "Heh, heh, heh."

A few minutes later his second steak arrived—very, very, rare and very, very tender.

The Family Reunion

Family reunions certainly are not uncommon, but in some instances they turn out much differently than anticipated. Such was the case of a family get together held in Western Howard County. Relatives from Tennessee, Kentucky, North Carolina and points south gathered to get reacquainted. To be sure, there were ample containers of alcoholic beverages to wash down the barbecue and other foods. Everyone in law enforcement knows that consumption of alcohol bolsters courage, lowers inhibitions, and often creates what is known as "beer muscles," causing some to believe they can whip Superman. At this reunion it was the women who first "flexed" their newly found beer muscles, and a cat fight ensued. Initially, the men were satisfied to cheer on the female combatants, but the inevitable punch was thrown, and all hell broke loose.

The host of the gathering, unable to quell the ever-growing brawl, called police. The first to arrive was Officer Richard Doxen, and upon seeing the size of the melee, he called for assistance. A familiar voice crackled over the radio and Corporal Robert "The Animal" Moore was on his way.

He arrived, looked the situation over, laughed and shook his head. He tried the PA system from the car, and the horn to get the attention of the fighters. Finally he turned on the siren, but the brawl continued. It was obvious to Bob and Officer Doxen that they were not going to be able to restore order—at least not in the conventional sense. And, it was just about this time that a very mangy cat wandered through the field of battle and settled atop the woodpile.

Bob turned to the homeowner. "Is that your cat?"

"No, it's some stray that showed up here, and the damn thing's been nothin' but trouble since it got here."

Bob grinned. "Heh, heh, heh."

In those days not much was said about the side arms worn on duty. Although the standard issued weapon at the time was the Smith and Wesson .38 caliber revolver; Bob was toting a Smith and Wesson .44 Magnum. He was lugging the original version of the "Dirty Harry" Model with the 6½-inch barrel. As the fight continued to grow, Bob drew the cannon from its holster. As casually as though standing on the firing line at the pistol range, he took aim and blew the cat off the woodpile.

The roar of the big magnum rose well above the din of the battle and immediately caught everyone's attention. Pugilists and wrestlers alike stopped and turned their heads in the direction of the grinning policeman, who still clutched the smoking cannon in his right hand. With silence now hovering over the field of conflict, Bob bellowed, "Now, what the hell's the matter?"

Without uttering so much as a single word, former antagonists were quickly seated side by side, eating beef, drinking beer and engaging in somewhat pleasant conversation. Bob holstered his revolver and walked back to his car. He looked over at the host. "Heh, heh, heh. I thought you had a fight here. I don't see a fight, do you?"

The host turned to Officer Doxen and muttered, "Jesus Christ. Nobody in their right mind's gonna fight with that crazy s.o.b. runnin' around loose."

The Xerox Phantom

When word began circulating that the Howard County Police Department was thinking of replacing its copy machine, companies quickly beat a path to the door, hoping to get the contract. Each offered a copy machine, free of charge, for up to a full week to demonstrate its capabilities. The game of One-upsmanship began in earnest, and finally Xerox delivered a machine, the likes of which nobody in the department had ever seen before. This copier offered some eye raising features, and the salesman boasted that it could make prints from 8½ x 11 up to poster sized copies. None other than Corporal Robert "The Lizard" Moore, the Night Shift Duty Officer, would immediately put the Xerox boast to the test.

The following morning, police officers, radio dispatchers and secretaries arriving for work were warned that The Xerox Phantom had struck sometime during the night. Copies of an "unknown" party's buttocks were on display everywhere. From restrooms, to desk drawers, to holding cells and the radio room, The Phantom's cheeks were bared in various sizes.

Chief of Police, Russ Walters opened the door to his office and was greeted with a poster-sized copy of the mystery cheeks, which were tacked prominently above and behind his chair. Scrawled in red letters, with a red arrow pointing downward were the words, "KISS MY."

Chief Walters hurried back into the lobby and shouted, "There's a copy of somebody's backside hangin' behind my desk."

It was almost an hour before a somewhat normal order returned to the police station. And, it was at that time one of the secretaries noticed that just below the "eye-catching" cheeks was just a hint of shorts, which displayed cute little valentine hearts.

Bob winked at the secretary. "Guess I'll hafta go home and burn my shorts."

But, before leaving, Bob had one last thing to do. It was one of those temptations that no matter the level of self-discipline, he just had to do it. He knocked on the door and stuck his head into office of Russ Walters and said, "Chief, you gonna call for a lineup to see if you can ID the culprit?"

"Moore, get your ass outta my office and go home."

Come Blow Your Horn

Bob began his law enforcement career in the City of Baltimore, Maryland, and it was there that the legend of "Sweet Bobby" began to take shape. On a steamy, sweltering summer's afternoon, he was ending his tour of duty and thinking of nothing but leaving the city and finding peace and quiet and some relief from the brutal heat. The thought of sitting in the shade with a cold drink seemed like a good idea. He got behind the wheel of his '56 Chevy and headed out Franklin Street and its endless maze of traffic signals. Minding his own business, he followed the steadily growing stream of commuters west toward the county. Not long into his trek he noticed a car rapidly bearing down on him, and suddenly it seemed as if it was glued to his bumper. Try as he might, he couldn't get the car off his rear end.

"I really think the s.o.b. was trying to get in the back seat," Bob would later say.

In no time at all, the man behind him wasn't satisfied with simply tailgating. He began to blow his horn—not now and then, but constantly, and especially at traffic lights. The very instant a traffic signal turned green, he laid on the horn. Bob was beginning to steam under the collar, and when he began to boil, it was time to get out of his way. For those who knew him, it was easy to read the telltale sign that "Sweetness" was starting to get riled. Bob's skin would change color, and the deep red would rise in his neck. Like a temperature gauge, you could read his degree of agitation. The higher the red climbed, the more pissed off he was becoming. When red hit the tops of his ears, he had been pushed beyond his limit of endurance, and his tormentor was going to endure the wrath of "The Animal."

The man continued to hammer the horn, and the incessant "honk, honk, honk" had taken its toll on Bob.

His temperature gauge had reached its boiling point, and he wouldn't tolerate another minute of this aggravating man and his honking horn. He stopped at the next red traffic signal and waited. The light turned green and, right on cue, the man slammed his hand down on the horn. Instead of driving on, Bob turned off the engine and got out of his car. An instant later he was walking toward his source of irritation, and the man had no place to go. He was hemmed in by the evening traffic.

Bob didn't confront the driver, at least not immediately. He paused and opened the hood of the man's car, reached down with his bear sized hands, wrapped them around the horns and ripped them from the car. It was a certainty that the look on his face was sending a very clear message to the man behind the wheel as he walked to the driver's door. He shoved the horns through the open window and held them just inches from the man's face. A moment later he dropped them in his lap and said, "Here, blow 'em now."

The man was still sitting at the traffic light as Bob drove away smiling, and surely enjoying some of the peace and quiet he'd been day-dreaming of.

Traffic Stop to Gunfire

On a Friday evening, Bob was patrolling the roads of West Friendship in Howard County, approaching the intersection of Sandhill Road. He watched a car roll through the Stop Sign and speed up, kicking up gravel and squealing wheels. Bob thought he'd stop the car, write the driver a warning, and send him on his way. When he activated the overhead lights, the driver accelerated and raced westward along Frederick Road to Route 32. At the intersection he turned left, cutting off several cars, hoping to elude his pursuer. He had traveled almost a mile when he cut sharply to his right and began fleeing down a narrow dirt road. Bob was right on his bumper as they bounced over the unpaved surface toward the parking lot of a private club. The car slid to a stop and the driver jumped out, but was surprised to find Bob already blocking his path to the club.

Bob immediately recognized the man, and knew he had no respect whatsoever for police officers. But, he followed protocol to the letter, and asked for the man's driver's license and registration. A heartbeat later, Bob found himself looking into the barrel of a small caliber handgun. He didn't even blink. Instead he looked the man squarely in the eyes and smiled. "Heh, heh, heh. You don't really think you're gonna kill me with that, do you?"

Bob's actions and comments must have caused the man to have second thoughts. For a moment he seemed puzzled, and then, for some unknown reason, he turned the gun and stared at it. In those seconds of uncertainty, the "Bear in Blue" pounced with the quickness of a cat. Bob hurled the man to the ground and tore the gun from his hands. A ham-sized fist crashed into the side of the man's head a half dozen times, knocking him senseless.

When Bob looked up, he found that a crowd of more than a hundred people surrounded him, and many of them were friends of the man lying at his feet. What he did next would surely be considered nothing short of complete insanity, but he grinned. Then he leaned over, grasped the front of the man's jacket and pulled his head from the ground.

"Wanna hear what your gun sounds like?" he growled. With that he took the man's gun, held it beside his right ear and fired. "Would you like to hear it again?" He held it beside his left ear and fired again. "Heh, heh, heh. How'd it sound?" He fired two more shots, one beside each ear.

Glancing over his shoulder, he found that the crowd had moved a considerable distance away from him. He rolled the man over, handcuffed him and stuffed him in the back of his cruiser as other police officers began arriving.

Without coaxing, the majority of the crowd went back inside to continue partying. Those who remained outside laughed, and talked with police officers about the crazy s.o.b. that had fired the shots.

In the end, the man who pulled the gun on "Sweetness" was sentenced to six months in the county jail. At the trial there was no mention of the shots that had been fired, and no one filed a formal complaint, or made so much as a single telephone call about what happened that night.

A Case of Mistaken Identity

The four men passing by Parker's Drive-in on U. S. Route 40 were certain that the policeman with the reddish-blonde hair, standing on the parking lot, was the one they had been searching for. They had a grudge to settle and figured this was a perfect time. After all, they had him outnumbered. They parked their car, and a moment later began their attack on him. Almost immediately it was evident that they had jumped the wrong man.

The only similarity between this policeman and the one they'd been searching for was the reddish-blonde hair and his height of five feet ten inches. This man in blue weighed 210 pounds plus, and had a fist the size of a Smithfield Ham, or the hoof of a Clydesdale. Then there was this very strange laugh he had. They were stunned that he actually laughed when they pounced on him, screaming they were going to kick his ass. Very soon they found themselves on the wrong side of the ass kicking.

Maryland State Trooper Pete Edge was dispatched to assist a Howard County Officer who was fighting four men. He skidded to a stop on the parking lot of Parker's Drive-in, leaped out of his car and stopped in his tracks. Indeed, there was a policeman there, but he was rather handily pummeling the snot out of three men. He stopped beating the three men long enough to look over at Pete and say, "Can I help you?'

Pete shrugged. "I was told you needed help?"

"Heh, heh, heh. I don't need any help." And, with that, Bob proceeded to pound away on the three men again.

"I was really thinking about leaving, when somebody reached out from under a car and grabbed my legs. I looked down and here's a guy with cuts all over his face and a bloody nose, and now he's wrapping his arms around my legs." Pete laughed. "I tried to shake him off, but he wouldn't let go. That's when I realized this guy had to be the fourth suspect."

As Pete tried to pry him from his legs, the man kept yelling, "Help! It's not that animal that needs help. It's us. Please don't leave. Help! Help us."

The Other Side

During his career Bob often seemed larger than life, and was a hero to so many who knew him, because he dared to stand his ground when others would flee. He gave no quarter when it came to enforcing the law, and firmly believed it was for everyone, rich or poor, black or white.

There was another side to Bob that only a select few had the opportunity to see. I was blessed to be one of those few. He would go out of his way to help children, regardless of their age. They seemed to always sense that the smiling, bear-like man had a heart of gold, and I am certain they knew that he would always watch out for them.

There was an occasion many years ago when I attended a Sunday morning Judo exhibition at a local health club. Bob, who had earned a Black Belt in the art of Judo while in Japan, was invited to attend and participate if time allowed. The man who was demonstrating various throwing techniques had chosen a boy, 15 years of age, and far less skilled than he, to be his partner. Early on it was evident that this man was using the youngster as nothing more than a dummy for the purpose of showing off to the large number of women in attendance. Each time the boy landed hard on the mat, it seemed to bolster the man's already over inflated ego. I looked at Bob and knew he detested what the man was doing. With every new assault by the man on the almost defenseless 15-year-old, I saw Bob's thermometer glow a brighter shade of red. Suddenly, as the man continued his unmerciful thrashing of the boy, he began to shoot verbal insults at Bob. I don't know what possessed him to do it, but after a number of slurs, he invited Bob to step out and take the boy's place. Although this man was a head taller and clearly had a greater reach advantage, the moment Bob stared into his eyes he knew he'd made a grave mistake. Try as he might, he couldn't escape the wrath of the enraged Grizzly. Bob threw him around the mat as though he was nothing more than a paper doll. When he slammed him to the mat for the final time, Bob dropped like a rock on top of him and choked him unconscious. As Bob left the mat, the young boy nodded and bowed to him.

"Sweetness" flashed him a big grin as he walked over, patted him on the back and returned his bow.

When he wasn't watching out for the local kids, or protecting the citizens of Howard County, Bob pursued his favorite hobby: hunting. He was an avid hunter who not only hunted locally, but also various states across the country. But his hunting skills weren't used merely to fill his freezer with game, or bag a trophy. He put meat on the tables of many less fortunate people, but never made his efforts known and, in fact, was just as happy helping others without the fanfare.

There is a small group of us who know the value and meaning of true friendship, and the days we spent acting as Guardian Angels for each other. We still find time to share with Bob and a few of our brothers from bygone days, and reminisce of high-speed chases, close calls, and friends who left us too soon. We laugh over a drink while spinning those yarns of "Sweet Bobby," our daring exploits and a few astounding deeds. When it's time to part, there's a round of handshakes and hugs, and the satisfaction of knowing we've held a friendship that's lasted a lifetime.

As for enemies, and as is the case with all of us, only the passing of time seems capable of wearing down the bear of a man so many of us know as "Sweet Bobby." I've often tried to picture his Lord and Maker knocking and announcing, "Okay, Sweetness, it's time to come home." And I can't help but imagine Bob smiling, turning out the light, closing the door, and responding, "Heh, heh, heh."

The Legend of
Robert "Sweet Bobby" Moore

About the Author

James Lilley is a former Marine and highly decorated twenty-five year veteran of the Howard County, Maryland Police Department. His awards include the Medal of Valor, four Bronze Stars, four Unit Citations and the governor's citation. Jim was selected as the 2008 Police-Writers.com Author of the year, and received an Honorable Mention for his book, The Eyes of the Hunter, in the New England Book Festival. The Eyes of the Hunter has also been adopted by Johns Hopkins University as required reading in the Master of Science in Intelligence Analysis program. Jim is also a lecturer at Johns Hopkins.

The Day Cambria Got Buzzed

By Steve Gilmore
(Second Runner-Up)

I had heard "the story" many times when I was a kid growing up in the 1950's and '60's. Maybe I heard it at one of the annual Baillies family reunions at Chandler Park in Pardeeville. Maybe I heard "the story" at a square dance that my parents regularly attended. Or, maybe I heard it at any number of church or social gatherings.

But, this is 2009, and I still hear "the story" when I attend any event in Cambria or environs. Oh, the story? It's about the day Cambria got buzzed by a Boeing B-17 heavy-duty military bomber, nicknamed the "Flying Fortress." My dad was the pilot and flying the brand new four-engine airplane and fully-equipped crew overseas to England to do battle with the Third Reich. The year was 1944.

I grew up in Waupun, Wisconsin, and my cousins on both sides of the family lived twenty miles away in the

Cambria area. My grandfather John (Jack), Aunt Jean, and cousins Terry and Linda, lived at the top of the hill on Scott Street. My Uncle Howard and Aunt MaeDonna lived on a farm halfway between Cambria and Rio. My cousins on the farm included Paul, Scott, Kelly, Kate Ann, and Joel. We got together often, and of course with my extended family, I had ample opportunities to hear "the story."

I had no doubt that the story was true, however, I wanted to record the eyewitness accounts of the buzzing of Cambria, before such verification is lost forever. My wife thought I was crazy and carried my research a bit too far, but this is what I can authentically document about the day Cambria got buzzed.

Both of my parents, June Baillies and Robert Gilmore, had graduated from Cambria High School. At the time of the attack on Pearl Harbor, my mom was working as a bookkeeper in Chicago and my dad was attending Platteville State Teachers College. He enlisted in the Army in January, 1942, and signed up for Aviation Cadet training. After a rigorous training regiment, on August 30, 1943, he received his "wings" and was commissioned 2nd Lieutenant Robert C. Gilmore – U.S. Army Air Corps.

Qualification as a pilot didn't end the training for the newly-commissioned officer. He completed the Four-Engine Pilot Transition Course at Roswell, New Mexico, and then moved on to the Combat Crew Training School at Ardmore, Oklahoma. It was at Ardmore, where all ten members of the flight crew on a B-17 trained together for the first time. Finally, at the end of February, 1944, the entire crew was transferred to the Processing Station – Grand Island, Nebraska, to prepare to fly overseas. It had taken two years to train these young men to join the largest armada of aircraft ever assembled and wage war with Hitler's Luftwaffe.

On March 8, 1944, Lt. Gilmore signed a receipt for a Boeing B-17G, serial Number 42-97206, and the crew conducted a test flight in order to calibrate instruments and check all equipment. On March 9th, crew members loaded the aircraft with government-issued necessities and limited personal effects, in preparation for their journey to England. The first segment of the trek was a flight from Grand Island, Nebraska, to Presque Isle, Maine. At five-o'clock in the morning on March 10, 1944, the four engines of the Flying Fortress came to life and she rumbled down the runway. As the big bird soared into the air, the pilot instructed the navigator to set a course for Cambria, Wisconsin.

It's been 65 years since Cambria got buzzed by this Flying Fortress, but there are still several eyewitnesses to the event. They have interesting recollections and different perspectives of "the story."

Tom (Buck) Williams said, "You know, barnstorming was popular before the war. They were stunt pilots who usually flew a small bi-plane. But barnstorming with a B-17? That's crazy."

Jean Rowlands was a teenager living on the hill near the high school. She remembers that "we heard a rumble that intensified. We stepped outside and just caught a glimpse of this shiny airplane roaring down Main Street. It seemed to be driving on the ground, but oh, so fast. It came back over the high school and the churches. We could see someone waving from a window on the side. It was a silver airplane."

State Representative Eugene Hahn grew up about a mile east of the Everett Gilmore farm. Here's how he recalls the day ... "We were eating breakfast after the farm chores of milking the cows, feeding and watering the horses, and feeding the laying hens and hogs. The dishes started to rattle and the loudest roar we ever heard had us running out of the kitchen, and here was this biggest thing we ever saw flying right over our house. This huge plane circled around and the second time they flew over our house the man in the nose of the plane was waving to us. Oh, they seemed so low. The plane headed toward Cambria…low…and I believe everyone there had their dishes shaking too. My uncle nodded his head and smiled, as he explained…B-17 boys…Bob Gilmore's on his way to war."

Renowned author John Steinbeck must have also experienced the shaking from these bombers. He wrote a book entitled <u>Bombs Away</u> which was published in

1942. It is the story of a bomber team and describes the training and responsibilities of each member of the flight crew. The very last paragraph of the book reads as follows: "The thundering ships took off one behind the other. At 5,000 feet they made their formation. The men sat quietly at their stations, their eyes fixed. And the deep growl of the engines shook the air, shook the world, and shook the future."

A great number of elders from the "Greatest Generation" are no longer with us. Those are the folks who grew up during the Great Depression, and became young adults during World War II. Indeed, my father, Robert Gilmore, died in 1968, and my mother, June (nee Baillies) passed away in 2006. I wanted to record the reactions of eyewitnesses who had experienced "the day Cambria got buzzed" before, they too, are gone.

Then it dawned on me…*wait a minute, you're only getting one perspective…from the folks on the ground. What about the crew in the air?* Well, I dug out an old scrapbook that my dad had made about his stint with the Army Air Corps. 'Lo and behold, I discovered a copy of a diary which had been maintained by the navigator of the crew. The diary begins on March 10, 1944 (the day Cambria got buzzed) and ends on August 8, 1944, the day the crew completed their required thirty-five combat missions.

March 10, 1944, was the crew's first segment of their flight across the North Atlantic to England. They took off from Grand Island, Nebraska, with a destination of Presque Isle, Maine. Here is the entry in the diary: "Departed Grand Island at 05:01, in the clear cold of the morning, with a full crew, as follows:

- 2nd Lt. Robert C. Gilmore – Pilot. Cambria, Wisconsin.

- 2nd Lt. Charles N. Baker – Co-Pilot. San Carlos, California.

- 2nd Lt. Robert A. Munroe – Navigator. Wichita, Kansas.

- 2nd Lt. Arthur W. Ordel – Bombardier. Lexington, Virginia.

- S/Sgt. Robert S. Walters – Engineer/Top Turret Gunner. Bayville, New York.

- S/Sgt. Milbert E. Maisch – Radio Operator/Gunner. South Dakota.

- Sgt. Charles G. Whittleder – Ass't. Engineer/Waist Gunner. Chicago, Illinois.

- Sgt. James M. Stewart – Waist Gunner. Clarksdale, Mississippi.

- Sgt. Fred M. Anderson, Jr. – Ball Turret Gunner. Gainesville, Texas.

- Sgt. Tom P. Coburn – Tail Gunner. Memphis, Tennessee.

Set course for Cambria, Wisconsin. Most of the crew indulged prolifically in a sack workout during the early hours of the flight. We came through undercast at 4,500 feet while crossing the Ole' Miss and proceeded to Cambria, where the old man indulged in a bit of low level flying at said town and also his homestead. Casualties to crew were none, but otherwise consisted of:

- 1 – shattered board fence at Billy Williams' place caused by a herd of rampant sheep following their leader through same.
- 1 – missing weather vane from Welsh Church – Cambria.
- 1 – dead hen at Gilmore's, who failed to get out of the prop blast.
- 865 sets of shattered nerves in Cambria.

By this time, the entire crew was well awake, and a few members participated in a bit of penny-ante, while navigator Munroe started to slowly freeze in the nose. The remainder of the trip was uneventful."

So, I had one account of "the story" as experienced from the air. I wondered if Navigator Bob Munroe was still alive. It has been 65 years since that young man made the entry into his diary. What about the rest of the crew? I decided to find out, and my instincts told me that these members of the "greatest generation" usually, except for fighting World War II, didn't stray too far from home. After doing some research, I felt that I had some good leads regarding the crew's (or descendants) whereabouts.

It was time to make contact, but what would I say? I dialed the telephone number in Virginia and a male voice answered. "Hello, I'm trying to locate an Arthur Ordel, who served on a B-17 during World War II." The response was a chuckle, and "that was me."

Oh my 'gosh, I was actually talking to a member of my dad's crew. I told him who I was and that I was calling from Wisconsin. Another chuckle, and "ya know, we buzzed his hometown." I told him that I was aware of the incident.

Bombardier Art Ordel was descriptive, "I was in the plexiglass nose of that plane and I swear I could look into the second-story windows of the homes and buildings in that town. I had to call out where the utility poles were located ahead of us."

That was the recollection of a man now 88 years old, who immediately became a new found friend. I inquired about the status of the rest of the crew. He informed me that he regularly attends reunions, and that "Chuck" was alive and well. Chuck is Californian Charles Baker, the co-pilot. I asked about navigator Bob Munroe and learned that he had, just recently, passed away. In fact, Art Ordel and Charles Baker were listed as honorary pall-bearers at his funeral.

Art Ordel provided the pedigree for co-pilot Charles Baker in California. Without hesitation, I immediately called Chuck Baker, who answered "hello." Having a certain amount of respect for my elders, I asked "Is this

Charles?" There was a pause, then "yes." I identified myself, and then explained that I had just finished talking to Art Ordel. I think he was somewhat taken aback, and so was I, as here was the guy who sat next to my dad in the cockpit.

He said he was not used to being called "Charles." I responded, "Well Chuck, I understand you really wanted to fly fighters." Another pause, then a chuckle, "Well, yes, I sort of thought that was my calling." We continued our conversation, and I assimilated a most profound feeling of gratitude for these aviators, and members of "the greatest generation" who, as young men, flew off to war as part of a mass-produced Combat Replacement Crew. The odds of them returning unscathed were not very good, since the Eighth Air Force had the highest casualty rate and most POW's of any branch of U.S. military service in World War II.

Bombardier Art Ordel's mother was well aware of the dangers, and was bound and determined to accept the invitation to a farewell dinner for the officers before flying overseas. Mrs. Ordel already had one son killed-in-action and she wanted to meet the fellows with whom Arthur would be flying over Nazi Germany. Other guests included Bob Munroe's wife, and Bob Gilmore's fiancée June. At the dinner, hosted by navigator Bob Munroe's parents in Wichita, Mrs. Ordel presented each aviator with a handmade white silk scarf.

The aircraft that they were flying had also been mass-produced and recently rolled off the assembly line at the Boeing plant in Seattle, Washington, where a majority of the workers were women, affectionately called "Rosie the Riveter." It was a large silver (unpainted aluminum) airplane with a 100-foot wingspan and four engines that produced 1,200 horsepower each. It was this airplane, traveling northeast, that descended over Rio in the Township of Springvale on March 10, 1944, and roared pass the Gilmore farm in order to buzz Cambria. Those flying the B-17, proudly wore their government-issue brown leather jackets and a white silk scarf.

Co-pilot Chuck Baker had also kept a diary and here's how he recorded the event: "Took off Grand Island in the clear crisp morning at 05:01. At about 09:00, we passed over Bob Gilmore's house in Cambria, Wisconsin (incidentally, I had to look up at the street signs). Landed at Presque Isle, Maine at 15:10, after being in the air ten hours and ten minutes. 'Twas exceptionally cold."

Subsequently, this crew would fly to the United Kingdom via Labrador, Iceland, and Scotland. Upon arrival at Prestwick, Scotland, the boys were immediately relieved of their shiny new silver ship with nary a blemish, by the Eighth Air Force officials who had a master plan. They had simply been the delivery boys.

After a month of additional training in the European Theater of Operations, they were assigned to the 390th Bomb Group stationed at Framlingham, England. The boys inherited a veteran war machine in an olive-drab B-17 with the name *BOMBOOGIE* stenciled on her nose in bold yellow letters. Together, they completed thirty-five combat missions and were awarded the Distinguished Flying Cross.

The citation, in support of the medal, reads as follows: "For extraordinary achievement while serving as pilot of a Flying Fortress on numerous bombardment missions in the air offensive over enemy occupied Continental Europe. Under the duress of heavy fighter attacks, anti-aircraft fire, and often under adverse weather conditions, Lieutenant Gilmore, by his superior airmanship, contributed to the success of all these operations. The untiring effort, skill, and determination under stress of combat displayed by Lieutenant Gilmore are in keeping with the highest traditions of the Army Air Forces of the United States."

Indeed, they had endured the wrath of the Luftwaffe and had many harrowing moments. Flak, those pesky puffs of inverted Ys that dotted the sky, was a frightening experience. The German anti-aircraft artillery units were accurate and when those shells burst, the jagged shrapnel radiated outward at the velocity of a speeding bullet that easily tore through the aluminum skin of a B-17 and penetrated anything or anybody contained therein. The German fighter pilots were experienced and also wreaked havoc as they barrel-rolled through the bomber formations. But a Flying Fortress had a dozen fifty-caliber machine guns of her own and could defend herself. The gunners in *Bomboogie* were credited with many enemy aircraft destroyed.

Early in the war, the U.S. Commanders of the mighty Eighth Air Force had established the principles of strategic daylight bombing. They had the "secret" Norden bombsight that could precisely place the bombs on target. The targets they chose were oil refineries, railways, airdromes, submarine pens, factories, ball-bearing plants, transportation and communication lines. The intent was to incapacitate the Nazi war machine. Combined with the British Royal Air Force's nighttime bombing raids, the enemy would be under constant attack. In the spring of 1944, it was solely this vast air armada that was conducting offensive strikes against the German heartland, and Gilmore's crew had arrived just in time.

In an airman's mind, the most dreaded target in all of Germany was the Big B... Berlin, and all of its concrete fortifications housing anti-aircraft guns. The first raid to the capital city was in March, when Bob Gilmore was signing that receipt in Grand Island. Now, they were combatants and the crew would definitely receive their baptism under fire, as five of their first ten missions took them to Berlin. On their first raid to the Big B, one engine was shot out and they feathered the propeller, becoming a straggler and struggling to return to base, but they made it. On the second voyage to the capital city, the boys in *Bomboogie* learned that their crew of ten men in one airplane was a minute particle of the 1,000 heavy bombers streaming toward Berlin. On another mission they lost their wing man who was struck by flak and veered off with a wing on fire...no chutes reported. Another time, both Walters in the top turret and Coburn in the tail, received credit for confirmed enemy fighters destroyed.

Those masses of B-17 Flying Fortresses and B-24 Liberators had to be a spectacular sight for Allied personnel and a horrifying sight for the Axis, who knew that the foreboding formations would never be turned away. A Stars and Stripes reporter wrote, "Their march across the sky was slow and steady. I've never known a storm or a machine or any resolve of man that had about it the aura of such ghastly relentlessness. You have the feeling that even had God appeared beseechingly before them in the sky with palms stretched outward to persuade them back, they would not have had within them the power to turn from their irresistible course."

Deep penetrations into Germany, such as the raids to Berlin, were perilous and tiring. Although the Flying Fortress soared gracefully, it took strength and stamina to fly the beast. Therefore, Gilmore and Baker took turns at the controls, usually in half-hour shifts. Bombardier Ordel dropped his bombs in the proverbial pickle barrel and navigator Munroe always guided them home. And, *Bomboogie* herself, contributed to their success, as the war weary Framlingham Fortress sustained battle damage, but always returned to base. Most of their air time was over enemy occupied territory and these missions typically lasted ten hours or longer. These raids were certainly heroic, but what was their most memorable mission?

Remember the day Cambria got buzzed? That very first ten-hour flight from Grand Island to Presque Isle is undoubtedly reminisced the most of any mission flown. It has become a bit of folklore for the small village in central Wisconsin. At the time of the buzzing, most young men were wearing the uniform of one of the U.S. military services. That meant that many young women were in the work force, doing what the young men would otherwise be doing. The older generation, veterans of World War I, contributed in significant ways. There was rationing and there were many sacrifices. The country was united in a common cause: Good versus evil.

When the boys descended over Cambria that day, they were a bit giddy, like college boys pulling a prank. In reality, they were insightful in their demonstration of pride and patriotism. All were aware of the hardships that others endured. All were aware of the tyranny that must be defeated. All were aware that America, the great melting pot, was emerging as the world's peacekeeper. And, all were aware of each other's courage. It was time to show the hometown folks the men and machines that were being produced to defeat the epitome of cruelty and barbarism. They probably had read about a B-17 in a newspaper or had seen a cinema newsreel, but this would be a first-hand look at a Flying Fortress up close and personal. She was a striking symbol of strength, freedom, and unwavering determination. Bob Gilmore and crew were on their way to war and would return victorious.

Six months later, 1st Lieutenants Gilmore and Munroe were aboard a different kind of ship, the U.S.S. Wakefield, a pre-war luxury ocean-liner converted to a troop transport carrier, returning to the United States. They were decorated soldiers, veterans of 35 combat sorties, and no longer boys. Bob Gilmore wrote a letter to his fiancée that would be hand-delivered. Bob Munroe pulled out his diary and there hadn't been an entry since August 8th, the date of their last mission. He flipped back to the beginning and read the passage from March 10th, the day Cambria got buzzed. He smiled and reflected that they were filled with anxiety, but eager to get on the business at hand.

He contemplated, and on September 4, 1944, he recorded his final comments in the journal:

"Aboard boat headed for those golden shores…the trip itself is boring…just water, water everywhere. Now is a good time to close out this log. I believe that we have been more or less typical of all bomber crews. We'd sweat out flak and fighters and they tired us, but more often what really wore us out was a struggle with an oxygen mask, creeping turret, runaway prop, or squeaky interphone. None of us were military minded, but crew discipline is something we never worried about. We led the squadron more times than any other crew in the group. We had some sort of innate attachment for our ground crew chief

M/Sgt. Ed Collins, the armorer, and the bunch of boys who worked on *Bomboogie*. We never doubted their advice concerning the mechanics of the plane, whether it was the plug in a flak hole of a wing tank or an engine change. They knew their stuff as evidenced by the fact that when we left the group, *Bomboogie* had 55 rough missions under her belt, and her guns had accounted for seven positive kills.

On the other hand, we weren't so typical as lots of crews, for we were a "lucky" outfit. Never were we forced to bail out, crash land, or ditch in the channel or North Sea. On the Magdeburg mission, half of the boys in our barracks didn't come back. In the hut where we sacked it, we were the only crew to complete our tour of duty. I wish those there now better fare."

1st Lieutenants Chuck Baker and Art Ordel had decided to stay in England and fly non-combat assignments while still receiving flight pay. Most of their flying jobs were to "slow-time" B-17s which had sustained major damage and had been repaired. In fact, as part of their slow-time job, they flew Gilmore and Munroe to Liverpool in order to embark to the USA. Baker recalled that it was not a bad gig and he even got to celebrate the liberation of Paris after the city rid itself of the oppressors. He flew crucial supplies to Patton's rapidly advancing Third Army…and stayed for a week!

Eventually, in 1945, the Allied Armed Forces achieved victory, in part due to the efforts of the thousands who served in the Eighth Air Force. They set the standard, and raised the bar high, for the generations of American militia who followed. British Prime Minister Winston Churchill stated, "In the British and American bombing of Germany and Italy during the war, the casualties were over 140,000…These heroes never flinched or failed. It is to their devotion that in no small measure we owe our victory."

There are undoubtedly thousands of contemporaneous tales of heroism that deserve to be told. There are also thousands of 8th Air Force airmen who did not survive World War II. Nowadays, if you see an octogenarian in the check-out line at a grocery store, engage them in conversation, as chances are they are a true American hero. While I cannot, in good consciousness, nominate an entire generation for unheralded accolades, I can validate that two new old friends, or two old new friends, are worthy of the honor:

Capt. Charles N. Baker, USAAF Ret. (age 89)
1st Lt. Arthur W. Ordel, USAAF Ret. (age 88)

The boys in *Bomboogie.* As John Steinbeck had predicted, they "shook the air, shook the world, shook the future." They are true American heroes!

The Day Cambria Got Buzzed

About the Author

Steve Gilmore is a thirty-five year veteran of the Dane County Sheriff's Office in Madison, Wisconsin. He has a Bachelor of Science degree in Criminal Justice from Milton College. He served six years in the United States Marine Corps – Reserve with an honorable discharge.

Steve graduated from the F.B.I. National Academy in 1983 (134th Session). He also graduated from the Hazardous Devices School and previously served as the Bomb Squad Commander. He is currently serving as a Lieutenant in the Investigative Services Bureau.

My Brother, My Hero

By Mark Lambert
(Finalist)

It was over 25 years ago when I first heard my brother say that he wanted to be a cop. My brother had been an EMT and a volunteer firefighter and I was already proud of him. When he was an EMT, I went on some ride-alongs with him and witnessed just how much he enjoyed helping people. When my brother graduated from the police academy and was hired by the Sheriff's department, it was the happiest day of his life. My brother quickly gained respect from his bosses, fellow officers and the community. His dedication to the badge showed in the long hours he worked, volunteering to work on his days off and just about every overtime opportunity that came along. My brother volunteered his own time when his shift was over or came in on a day off to work certain cases that occurred in his area. His dedication usually resulted in several felony arrests that helped close many felony cases.

My brother asked me to go on a ride-along with him one night and I was hooked. I witnessed his enthusiasm first hand with his desire to help people and to put criminals behind bars. Seeing my brother's satisfaction and dedication got me thinking about becoming a police officer. I took some classes and became a reserve officer and quickly realized the same satisfaction that my brother was always talking about. I volunteered several days a week as a reserve officer for 2 years and decided to become a full time officer. My department put me through the police academy and, on the day I graduated, my brother pinned my new badge on my uniform. As we looked into each others teary eyes, we both felt an enormous sense of pride.

I started my new career which put a strain on my family life. Cops do not have set working hours or days, and there is no such thing as nights, weekends or holidays off; at least at the beginning of a cop's career. Luckily, I have an understanding wife and was still able to be a big part of my children's lives as they grew up. My brother's dedication to police work and the long hours also took a toll on his relationships. My brother was never able to sustain a long term relationship due to his desire to work. We both worked the "graveyard" shift and we would always check up on each other to make sure the other was safe. If a call came out where my brother was working, I knew he'd probably be the first one on scene. The risk of police work worried both of us but the satisfaction we felt was worth the risk.

When I started my police career, my brother was a canine officer with a 140 lb Rottweiler. As soon as I was eligible to become a canine officer with my department I jumped at the chance. I started working with a 125 lb Rottweiler that was actually a sibling to my brother's Rottweiler. My brother was there to help me get started and we often trained together. I was at my brother's side when he had to put his beloved partner to rest, both of us with tears in our eyes. Several years later, my brother was at my side when I had to put my partner down due to cancer; again, with tears in both of our eyes.

Some say that cops don't cry and that cops get so hardened and cynical that they don't show emotion. Cops do cry; they just hold it inside and cry alone. I always saw my brother with a smile on his face, but after becoming a cop, I know that the calls involving young children, the elderly or tragic accidents took their toll, even if cops don't show it on the surface.

As our careers continued, we both went into different job assignments. My brother went into the marine patrol unit and later the air support unit. I always knew to expect a visit from my brother when I'd make a traffic stop or go to a "hot" in-progress call. There would suddenly be a helicopter circling overhead with a spotlight making it look like daytime. It got to the point where other officers assisting me on calls would hear an approaching helicopter and say "here comes your brother". It was nice knowing my big brother was watching over me while I worked. During my career, I lost two fellow officers and friends at my department who were killed in the line of duty. While standing at attention at both of their funerals; I had tears running down my face as several helicopters flew overhead in the missing man formation. My brother was in one of those helicopters with tears running down his cheeks too. Attending a cop's funeral is a very emotional experience and we both knew that could have been a funeral for either one of us.

While we continued in our careers, no matter where I went, I always heard good things about my brother. I learned a lot from my brother and I learned to treat everyone with respect, even the bad guys. I came to this realization one day when I took a man to jail who was looking at several years of confinement. As we pulled into the jail entrance, the man thanked me. Not a sarcastic thank you, it was a genuine thank you. I asked the man why he was thanking me when I was taking him to jail, probably for a long time, and I'll never forget what he said. The man told me: "I know I did wrong and I deserve whatever I get. You treated me with respect and respect is the only thing I have left in my life. If you had tried to take my self respect away I would have fought with everything I had. But you treated me like a man and gave me respect. Even though you are taking me to jail, I want to thank you for treating me with respect." I will remember that day throughout my career.

My brother always tells me how proud he is of me but it is I who is the most proud. Thanks to my brother, he showed me what a hard work ethic is, what dedication is, what respect is. We are both still street cops and see each other occasionally, but we don't keep in contact with each other as much as we used to, or probably as much as we should. I still continue to hear nothing but good things about my brother. If there really is such a thing as a cop's cop, it is my brother. My brother will always be my hero.

My Brother, My Hero

About the Author

My name is Mark Lambert and I am a police officer in Northern California. I have been with the same police department for almost 20 years. I have worked different assignments including patrol, investigations, K-9, motors and juvenile.

I have been married to a very understanding wife for 27 years and I have two wonderful daughters, one who has given me a new joy in my life; a grandson. While police work takes its toll on most marriages, I was lucky enough to have a very supporting and understanding family.

MY HERO JIM

By Jody Lilley
(Finalist)

My hero is my husband, James H. Lilley. I worship the ground he walks on and live for him every day. He attended Catholic Schools, went to Leonard Hall Military School in Southern Maryland and then attended Mount Saint Joseph's in Irvington, Maryland. These schools instilled in him a strong sense of duty and discipline, and he graduated with top grades. He also developed a fondness for the military, especially the Marine Corps.

Jim's father owned a very successful insurance company and the plan was for Jim to take over the business, but Jim had other plans. Jim wanted to follow in the footsteps of his uncles who fought so valiantly in the Marine Corps during WWII, so he enlisted. Jim's father wasn't exactly pleased with his decision and told him the government could now pay for his food.

The Marines made a man out of Jim. During a deployment to Okinawa, Japan in 1963, Jim befriended a fellow Marine by the name of Len. The two had a strong interest in learning karate and they asked a taxi driver if he knew of perfect place in which to study. The driver took them down a dirt road and introduced them to Takeshi Miyagi. As the two Marines began learning this ancient art, the Okinawans in the class did everything they could to get the Americans to quit, but this did not happen.

As time went on, friendships grew and so did trust. Jim and Len trained hard and ultimately both men were awarded their black belts, which was a first, since no American had ever received a black belt rank from Mr. Miyagi.

Time passed and Jim became a well-decorated police officer with the Howard County, Maryland Police Department, rising to the rank of sergeant. It was said many times that if a dirty job needed to be done, call on Sgt. Jim Lilley to do it. Though Jim retired from police work after twenty five years of service in 1992, he is still called on regularly for advice. In fact, many commanders in jurisdictions throughout Maryland look up to Jim as a leader. At a recent police funeral, the presiding priest quoted Jim, "That it takes a true leader, such as Jim Lilley, to lead the way for others." I wish I were there to hear these words, because I was told that the commanders had their heads down when the priest spoke and these commanders were not praying at the time.

As time went by in the department, many of the people that worked for Jim were promoted. Most of the people would tell me that the learned from the master, "Sergeant James Lilley" on how to be the proper supervisor and worked the squads, platoon and sections the way Jim would. Jim is still regarded and looked up even to the young kids in the academy to this day. It was said, the day that Sergeant Lilley retired in 1992, a legend left, but will never be forgotten.

In September 1992 a terrible carjacking occurred in Howard County, Maryland. Dr. Pamela Basu was killed when two men from Washington, D.C. stole her car and dragged her to death. The sheriff of the county was responsible for the courtroom security during the one trial. The first and only person he could think of to run the security was Jim Lilley. He knew that Jim on the assignment, everything would be secure and with no problems would happen. It was not an easy trial, but the operation of everything was smooth as could be. I had to testify in the trial and I told Jim that I would feel safer with him in the room and surer of myself. With him there, it was as if I was testifying to a traffic ticket.

As Jim's wife, I love him with all my heart and would follow him to the end. He has helped me become the person I am today. Growing up, I was never scared of much, but after meeting him, taking his karate class and believing in myself, I know I can do what ever I put my mind to. A published author, Jim occasionally gets hurt when he receives a letter that his books are not well written, or he needs an agent to submit work, but I just give him a big hug and tell him I believe in him and someday, he will be looking down on all the people that have been looking down on him. I tell him to forget all the negativity out there, but most of all I tell him 'I love you will all my heart.' My husband is the best husband there is. I love him and, before I retired, I could not wait to come home and see him. I hated leaving him in the morning or during my last four years of work at night. He is my world, my life, and my best friend.

My Hero Jim
About the Author

My name is Jody Ann Lilley. I have been married to James Lilley since December 2, 1992. We have known each other since February 6, 1988. That is the night of our first date. However, I had known him since May 1983, which is when I became a police dispatcher with the Howard County Police Department, Maryland. From that day forward on meeting Jim, I knew he would be the one for me. I really liked his rugged looks and just the way he told things as they were meant to be told.

He introduced me to karate and made a believer out of me that I can do whatever I wanted to do with my life. We are 21 years apart in age but that does not even bother us. I love him for who he is and that is all that matters. Many have said they wished they had the relationship with their spouse like Jim and I do. We love doing the same things. If something does not interest the other, we go with the flow.

My father was in the Navy for 21 years and retired in Virginia. He accepted a job in Maryland in 1976 and that is what brought me to my new home state. With my new friends in high school, I learned about a Police Explorer Post 1952 and joined. I was in the post from 1978 to 1983 when I accepted the position of civilian dispatcher. I love Maryland and would not move even when my family moved to Pennsylvania in 1985. I had friends and a man that I knew one day would my husband to look after.

I became a police recruit in Howard County Police Department July 24, 1989 and graduated December 22, 1989. I was selected as a runner up for first year officer and told by my many classmates and hardened officers that I deserved the award and not the person whom received it. I was fourth runner up for Mid-Atlantic Female officer of the year in 1993, an honor that not too many of my fellow female officers have received, even to this day. I have been nominated as Police Officer of the Year and received many certificates and letters of recommendations. On April 30, 2008, I retired after 25 years of service as the rank of Sergeant. I worked on the night shift in the Southern end of the county that included the Jessup Truck Stop, Savage, Laurel and Columbia. I had the responsibilities of 6 individuals to deal with every night and enjoyed every minute of it.

Jim and I were not blessed with children of our own; he has a son from his first marriage and two wonderful grandchildren and a great daughter in law. Our children are the people that worked for our karate student's and us young and old and of course our animals.

Aldo and the Giant

By Mike Stamm
(Finalist)

There are factors other than rank and seniority that enter into decisions and actions by Michigan State Police. Some might describe the most prominent factor to be "forceful personality", while the less-tactful might simply refer to it as "who has the biggest set of balls".

Few in MSP acknowledge such a reality, while fewer still applaud its existence. An even-smaller minority have the insight and audacity to actually be such iconoclasts, and to thrive upon exerting influence from positions of low rank. This is not unique to MSP. Sweden's Military Intelligence is called "Unterrattelser" which literally means "correction from below". In some organizations, it is called "the tail wagging the dog". By road troopers, it is simply referred to as "getting things done".

Local ordinances are subject to state statutes, which are in turn subordinate to federal law. A good road trooper understands that above federal law, religious law, and natural law is Car Policy, as determined by his partner and him.

A solid road troop (an admittedly rare bird) might be described by other solid road troops as follows:

A good man, though not necessarily a nice man;

One with a refined sense of cosmic justice;

And one who will do anything *for* a friend, and anything *to* an enemy.

Aldo and the Giant

The troops approached the lounge warily, vehicle lights off and waiting quietly in the parking lot, windows down.

"Never been called here before. Paul runs a nice place, hardly ever gives us calls," said Sorenson, "especially involving drunked-up ex-pro football players."

"Semi-pro," corrected Smith. "Dispatch has no record of prior arrests on this guy," Looking intently toward the bar, he considered his own words and added, "Of course, they could be lying, just to screw us up. I'm betting he's big, anyway."

"Semi-big," said Sorenson archly. Nobody got in the last correction with him.

Aldo Sorenson was short for a troop, a scant fraction of an inch over the minimum five feet, nine inches, and compensated for it with massive strength and explosive aggression. Pugnacious and volatile, he had notably low tolerance for stupidity and bullies, and even less for subtlety and evasion. Those qualities, along with a relentless drive to say what was on his mind without considering the feelings of anybody, were generally considered to be attributes by his partners. The same qualities often put him at odds with command types and the rest of the universe. Aldo didn't mind, not for one second.

"Whaddaya think, Al?" demanded Smith. "Want to go see what's up?

"Nah. Gimme a minute to put on my sap gloves."

"Sure. Then we'll go reason with him," said Smith, still watching the building. "I have a new theory I'm working on," he continued, "I think that waiters judge what a person's like entirely by the tip he leaves. You know-- the guy could be Charles Manson and they'd say 'Well, trooper, a smelly little white guy with a swastika carved between his eyes came in and eviscerated all the customers and set the place on fire. Left a 25 percent tip. Great guy.' "

Al's face pinched skeptically, "You really think Chuck Manson'd tip 25 percent?"

"Not the point. The point is that waiters judge you by the last thing you do, which is leave a tip. Kinda like reverse-engineering-- you start with the result, and go backwards. Whatcha think?"

"I think your theories are screwy. You're the genius who had two theories about nurses-- that they're all sex maniacs, and that it's because they wear white pantyhose."

Smith nodded, "Those two need refinements, all right, but they still have potential. First of all, I didn't know your wife was a nurse when I came up with them. You think there's a possibility that sex maniac stuff only applies to them until they get married?"

"That's possible. At least with the guy they get married to."

"See? There you go," Smith said, brightening. "I'll put some more thought into that, and the white pantyhose thing, too," he added expansively. "What say we go see if somebody's in desperate need of an ass-whuppin'?"

They entered the lounge, dimly-lit and richly furnished with a great deal of dark wood and gleaming brass. Smith expected to be met by a scurrying, breathless career tattler, frantically pointing out the transgressor. Instead, the owner moved smoothly toward them, his relaxed air leading Smith to think they might have been dispatched to a false call. Paul was a dark, squat man in his late fifties who always dressed as though he was on his way to a family funeral, and greeted the two with professional politeness.

"He's a regular, usually comes in with his wife. Came in alone tonight, had a meal—

two, in fact-- and a couple martinis, maybe three. Got loud, started shouting at other customers, and was asked to leave. Waitress offered to call a cab for him and he grabbed her ass, instead. She split his lip. We don't want to press assault charges, we just want him out. Unless he gives you a bad time." This wasn't the first time he had dealt with responding officers, Smith suspected.

The owner pointed with his chin toward a corner booth near the kitchen door. "That's him over there. Said he won't leave until we serve him more drinks. Also said he'd tear the place apart if we called the police."

Al nodded once, pressed his hat tighter onto his head, and took a step toward the booth.

"Wait a second," said Smith. "One last question-- how does this guy usually tip?"

Paul shrugged. "Huge tipper, never less than 40 percent. He's also a huge asshole, though dealing with assholes is the cost of doing business. But he crossed the line when he touched my help. He's been told he's never welcome here again. Nobody comes in to my place and touches my help."

Al raised an eyebrow toward Smith, who massaged a temple with the fingertips of one hand. "Ah, well," he said dismissively, "no sense in putting any more effort into that one."

Sorenson rumbled directly toward the corner booth, locked on like a huge-asshole-seeking missile. The other patrons stirred nervously at their tables, whispering and shifting looks between the troops and the broad-shouldered man in the booth. They all avoided making eye contact with the troops, but were apparently too fascinated with events to leave. Al ground to a halt before the man, and stood silently until the man looked up into his face. The drunk rolled a vast paw protectively around his glass of melting ice, and growled like a dog over his food bowl.

Having eased up from the other side of the booth, Smith spoke first. "Evening, sir," he began in a neutral voice, "looks like we have a problem here."

The man broke his eyes from Sorenson, and turned them upon Smith. He was a wide, square-headed man, tie hanging loose at the open neck of his rumpled dress shirt, whose otherwise-wrinkled tailored suit was taut across his chest and arms. His hair was red, turning silver at the temples, cut well. He had a wide nose, bright with veins and showing signs of past violences visited upon it, and small bloodshot blue eyes set deeply beneath thick scarred brows. His lower lip was purple and swollen, and he sucked at it without apparent concern. When he spoke his voice was gravelly and slurred, but quite understandable.

"Fuck you, asshole," he said, gulping down his watery drink. "*You* got a problem." He slammed his empty glass to the table. "Me."

Smith smiled widely, tilting his head slightly to the side as though studying something of immense fascination to him. The man began to say more, but was interrupted by Sorenson thumping on the table with his gloved knuckles, then speaking.

"You. On your feet. Now."

Very deliberately, the man shifted attention back to Sorenson.

"You got it, shrimp. I'll stand up. Just remember, you asked for it."

"Sir," said Smith, voice low and oozing with mock concern, "I'm certain you're a real street-fighting maniac, you being a semi-professional ex-athlete and all. But seeing as you just got your ass handed to you by one skinny gal, do you *really* think this is the night you want to piss off a couple of Michigan state troopers?"

The man ground wide, yellow teeth together and stretched spatulate hands upon the table in simmering anger, and slowly stood. And stood.

"Al," said Smith quietly, watching the giant reach full height, "I'll admit my tip theory was way outta line. But your semi-big concept wasn't even close."

Aldo tipped his head back to maintain silent, glaring eye contact with the drunk, and Smith spoke in a voice he was certain would carry to the other tables. He was, he reminded himself, playing for an audience. "Sir. You've been asked to leave by this establishment's owner. If you refuse to leave, you will be committing a misdemeanor in our presence, and we will be forced to arrest you. Sir." A long pause. "What is your intent?"

The immense drunk's head swiveled slowly toward Smith.

"My intent?" he roared, his voice quavering with barely-suppressed rage, "My intent? I'll tell you my fuckin' *intent*, you shithead. First I'm gonna kick this shrimp's ass, and then I'm gonna kick yours." His turned his face back toward Al but stopped, confused, at the conversational tone of Smith's response.

"Oh, yeah!" Smith's face glowed happily. "I get it-- Boris Badenov, right? 'First we get moose. Then we get squirrel.' Man, I used to love that show. And *now*," he said dramatically, gesturing grandly toward Aldo, "watch my partner pull a rabbit out of his hat."

The drunk turned toward Al just in time to see him tuck his chin to his chest and crouch. Al exploded upward, an uppercut slicing into the drunk's crotch. Without hesitation, Aldo followed it with a left hook, then a right, low to the drunk's slack gut, paced as steadily as were he chopping wood. The drunk rolled back onto his heels, teetered, face purpling, then rose ponderously to his toes, emitting a tiny high-pitched squeal that reminded Smith of his grandmother's teapot. *Whoever could have expected that memory, here?* Smith found himself wondering.

The drunk's interminable squeal became ominously louder, then took on a liquid, gurgling quality. Both troops sprang back, the giant tipping forward over his overturned table, lurching from the corner and toward the other tables as though frantically seeking advice, then erupting into a technicolor stream of projectile vomiting. Nobody had to order the curious onlookers to move on-- they uprooted tables and jettisoned meals and drinks without a backward glance, scrambling toward the doors in abject panic as the drunk spewed noxious streams in all directions. He crashed onto a table and it splintered beneath him. He struggled weakly to extricate himself from the wreckage, then collapsed and was still.

"That was twice he called me a shrimp," said Sorenson, by way of explanation.

"Good enough for me, partner. But I suspect the charges should read something more along the line of 'Trespassing, Disorderly Person, and Hindering and Obstructing Police Officers'. Judges find it more impressive than 'Calling My Buddy Aldo A Shrimp'."

"Whatever. Man, that guy sure stinks."

"Yup. Glad he didn't do that in our car."

The owner edged into the room, a bit warily. "Is he dead?" he asked casually.

"Nah," said Smith, toeing the still form cautiously, "taking a little snooze, is all. It's been a big night for the lad."

Paul sadly surveyed the room, sniffing in disgust, as the troops gingerly handcuffed the vomit-smeared drunk's hands behind him and pulled him to his feet. Al grabbed an upper arm, and roughly steered the stumbling man toward the door.

"Sorry about the mess, here," said Smith, after taking the owner's information and putting away his pocket notebook.

Paul shrugged philosophically. "You know what they say-- can't make omelets without breaking some eggs. Your partner sure as hell broke that guy's."

"He did, that. Kinda put a damper on business, what with everyone shrieking and sprinting to their cars."

"It was getting late, anyway," Paul noted, shrugging again. "They'll all come back in a day or two, bring extra friends along to tell them the story. It all seems to even out. Anyway, thanks for taking care of this. Any customer pitches a bitch about police brutality, let me know and I'll be happy to clear up any misunderstanding. You guys did a neat job, here."

"I don't know that 'neat' is the word that springs to my mind," said Smith, wincing as he took in the carnage.

Shrug. "Hey. I learned a long time ago, you have to work with what you got. You can't make chicken salad out of chicken shit."

Smith pursed his lips as he contemplated Paul's last observation, then pulled his notebook from a rear pocket and added it to his notes.

"That one's worth remembering," Smith explained.

Smith walked to the patrol unit, finding the drunk snoring wetly in the back seat and Sorenson in the shotgun seat, scowling over paperwork.

"Ah," Smith said lustily, sliding behind the steering wheel. "There are those who object to the stench of vomit, but *I* consider it to be charming. I find this particular bouquet to be bold and piquant, with just enough sassiness to say 'I didn't smell all that good before being eaten, but since rotting in an alcoholic's stomach, I have something of great import that I *insist* I share with you'."

Aldo looked up from his paperwork, wide face smooth. "Fucker called me a shrimp. Twice."

"So he did. And paid dearly for it. You hungry, partner?"

"Sure. Soon as we dump this asshole and hose out the back of this car. Where we going?"

"I don't care. But for some reason, I have a craving for chicken salad."

THE CHRISTMAS CAROL PROJECT

By Mike Stamm
(Finalist)

Sipping beer and staring into campfires, troopers' stories reveal the qualities they most treasure. All agree that there is an immense difference between what is legal, and what is just. A good tale that includes elements of both justice and vengeance is particularly treasured, particularly when brought about by another policeman.

Not all troopers are pranksters, but most appreciate a good practical joke. Though not renowned for their sophisticated senses of humor, troops tend to most enjoy pranks with some level of appropriateness about them—jokes with a dash of cosmic justice, if you will.

An ideal prank has some level of complexity, as it gives the jokester the opportunity to demonstrate the depths of his deviousness, and any personal skills he can employ to make the joke more pungent are admired.

Some road trooper pranks are pulled on felons, while most are pulled on other troops. The best are directed toward command-types— "suits" who have shown they look down on road troops. Some suits are part of MSP's command, some from other organizations. All are equally despised.

Occasionally, a joke assumes a life of its own and involves more resources and time than could originally have been imagined, and moves the endeavor from the realm of mere prankhood. When all the elements can be properly aligned and the prank can be legal, just, and appropriate, such jokes evolve into Projects.

When they've been pulled and the target remains unaware he was a victim, they might even become legendary...

"You remember my buddy Jack Hanrihan, don't you, Smith?" asked Dave. The two were, once again, on pass and enroute to a non-MSP-sponsored training course.

"Sure. EA-6B pilot, Navy captain, condescending elitist, tightwad extraordinaire, abysmal pistol shot."

"You've got him pegged. I need some help on a little something involving Jack."

"What? He need something heavy lifted?"

"Nope. He got his ass in a crack, and I need some help pulling a prank on him. You in?"

Smith pulled upright behind the steering wheel, visibly brightening, and reached for his coffee cup.

"A prank? On Jack? You know I'm in. What did he do?"

"You've already mentioned what a stingy asshole he is. He calls it 'frugal', of course. Well, his wife finally conned him into taking her to a show in Norfolk, so she had an excuse to buy a new dress and see something other than the on-base hut they live in. Jack finally agreed and loaded her into their Impala to go to town, but being the notorious cheapskate he is they didn't park in a secure lot, because it would have cost him an extra five or six bucks."

"Jack's too smart to fall for that," nodded Smith.

"Yes, he is. So they go catch the show, and as they're heading back to their Chevy they spot an old black wino staggering down the opposite side of the street toward them. Jack, being a trained observer, says to his bride "That's funny. That guy is wearing a leather flight jacket like I keep in my car."

Smith began giggling maniacally in anticipation.

"And then he says, 'That duffel bag he's hauling looks a lot like the one I store in my trunk to hold all my old issued gear.'"

"Don't say it," interrupted Smith, "and that goof was actually shocked when he got to his car and found it had been burglarized."

"I was gonna say 'surprised', but I'm betting 'shocked' might be a bit closer to the truth," Dave admitted. "He called me in a rage, shouting about how he wished he'd never sold his handgun, because he'd be driving up and down the streets of Norfolk, Virginia blasting bums."

"Missing bums, the way he shoots."

"Anyway, I thought I'd pick up a blank Hallmark card, and you could help me put together something to tease him with."

"Har. Sure, I'll help. But this isn't just a prank-- there're way too many things coming together on this. We got Cap'n Jack the asshole, a theft from an auto, a street derelict, and you going south over the Christmas holidays. We might even have planetary alignments involved. You had it right when you first mentioned this. This isn't just a prank," he announced, "this is a *project*."

The two arrived at their class, where their instructor droned through the nomenclature portion of the course-- a seemingly endless litany of eminently forgettable names for obscure pistol parts. Dave struggled to remain conscious, while Smith scribbled furiously. Upon finally reaching mid-morning, Dave nudged Smith into awareness that the class was taking a break. The instructor nodded approvingly at Smith's intense desire to learn, and his obvious fascination with the finer details of the internal workings of autopistols.

"What the hell you doing, showing off?" demanded Dave. Smith tipped his head inquiringly, and Dave continued. "How the hell can you be so excited about nomenclature, for Chrissakes?"

"Nomenclature?"

"Parts' names-- nomenclature! You know, the stuff we've been studying all morning! What the hell you think I'm talking about?"

"Is that what they call this shit? I must not have been paying attention."

"So what have you been writing all morning, if not class notes?"

"It's a secret-- so highly classified that if I told you I'd be required by national policy to kill myself, and then kill you and all your idiot relatives." He squinted suspiciously over each shoulder before whispering conspiratorially, "Mum's the word. Loose lips sink ships. Floss daily, and brush after every meal." He scrutinized the room carefully before jabbing an accusing index finger at Dave. "You know," he said with finality.

"I know you're out of your mind," said Dave.

"Ha!" was Smith's only response, as he resumed his frenzied scribbling.

The instructor was a bit surprised when Smith, obviously his most dedicated pupil, suddenly stood during the next training session. Smith rummaged through his parka pockets until he extracted his car keys, then grabbed his immense mittens and burst, coatless, from the room. Smith was present at the conclusion of the next break, and sat through the remainder of the day's class quietly, no longer writing though apparently attentive.

When Dave and Smith opened the doors of Smith's car at the day's end, Dave reached in to move an envelope from his car seat. "Don't touch it!" shrieked Smith, before pulling a mitten onto his hand and carefully placing the envelope on his dashboard. He glowered at Dave to drive home his point, then headed to their nearby hotel. Upon arriving he again pulled on his mitten, then carefully carried the envelope at arm's length to their room.

Dave looked at the envelope from what he deemed to be a safe distance, and said, "You went to Hallmark when you ran from class this morning, and bought a blank card. Right?"

"Good eye, Pilgrim," admitted Smith as he pulled a new, wide-tipped marker from its package.

"Lemme guess. You didn't want your prints on it, so you marched into the card store with your arctic mittens and short-sleeved shirt, bought the card, and carried it out like it was a bomb."

"Wow, I'm impressed. You're really into this secret-agent shit, too, huh?"

"You're nuts." Dave craned his neck, "Now what are you doing?"

"Writing Jack a letter from his burglar. I'm doing it left-handed, in block letters, with plenty of inconsistent misspellings. It isn't perfect, but it isn't bad." He scowled briefly at his scribbled rough drafts. "Too many police words in it to fool him for very long. I figure it'll cause him a little anxiety for two or three minutes, max, then he'll figure out it's one of our stunts. Still, two or three minutes can be worth it."

"You're overestimating him," concluded Dave, reading Smith's work over his shoulder, "I predict he'll swallow this hook, line, and sinker. Jack thinks he's way too smart to fall for a joke, and he's really pissed off. This isn't bad, and it's gonna make him nuts. Maybe drive him to suicide."

Smith looked up from his laborious printing. "Cool," he said, and went back to work.

Stopping occasionally to shake cramps from his left hand, Smith finally finished writing on the blank card and addressing its envelope. He sealed the envelope's flap with a moistened washcloth ("No saliva-- DNA," was all he said) and then sealed it in a clear, larger envelope.

"When you fly south to your mother's next week, mail this to him."

"Got it. I'll drop it in a neighborhood mailbox in Atlanta on the way. Nothing close to my mom's, and nowhere near anyone we know. I'll toss the clear envelope somewhere else, and I won't touch the envelope he's getting." He carefully folded a paper bag over the envelope and added. "This is a masterpiece. He'll never figure we pulled one on him."

"That'd make it perfect. The funniest and cruelest pranks are the ones when the guys they're pulled on don't even know it. But I still think he'll know it was us."

"You don't have any idea how high an opinion he has of himself, or how low an opinion he has of us."

"That'd make it perfect," Smith repeated, nodding happily.

Several weeks later, Dave called Smith. "Jack called me today. He's coming into town tonight, wants to take us to dinner."

"Can't make it, partner. But let me know of any significant changes to Burger King's menu."

"No, he's serious. Needs our insight on the investigation of a mysterious letter he received from the guy who burglarized his car. He'll even take us to a nice place. Our choice."

"Get outta here."

"Real deal. He claims Naval Intelligence is investigating it." He chuckled. "I think he's serious."

"Naval Intelligence? If he was trying to B.S. us, why wouldn't he say FBI? You don't think he really fell for it, do you?"

"I think that if this was pulled on one of us, we'd come up with a massive counter-stunt. I think that he doesn't even entertain the possibility that he could ever fall for a joke." His drink's ice tinkled through Smith's telephone. "I'm telling you-- I think he fell for the whole prank."

"We'll see. Let's call around, find the most expensive restaurant in the area. And remember, it isn't a prank. It's a project."

"I remember. You just remember not to laugh."

Jack picked them up from Dave's house, where the two had met to solidify their plans for the night. They would listen politely to Jack's account, and offer only vague input. They would ask no questions of the incident or of Jack's actions, fearing they might inadvertently reveal information they would only the prankster might know. Above all, they would deny any involvement in the prank, even in the face of irrefutable proof.

"And remember, Smith," said Dave sternly, "no laughing."

"I shall strive manfully," swore Smith, "but I cannot make any promises. If I hold laughs in for too long, I could suffer life-threatening internal injuries."

Jack began his tale while driving to the restaurant. Smith was not surprised to find that the account was exactly as had been relayed by Dave. Unlike Smith, Dave had no natural tendency toward exaggeration and embellishment. Smith considered that a trait that indicated a lack of imagination, and was silently pleased that he suffered from no such predictability.

Jack mentioned receiving the letter, and his conclusions concerning it.

"It was obvious to me that the writer was intentionally disguising his handwriting," he said. "For instance, he used only capitalized block letters, and from the awkward slant I believe he was probably right-handed, but writing with his left hand."

Dave shot a reproachful glare toward Smith, who squirmed in the back seat.

"He was also probably much more educated than he wanted me to believe," continued Jack.

"How educated do you think he is?" asked Dave.

"I'd say he made it through fifth or sixth grade, anyway," Jack answered. Smith nodded somberly.

"The letter mentioned things I initially thought he shouldn't have known," said Jack. "For instance, it mentioned me by my nickname, 'Jack', instead of my given name, 'John'. It eventually came to me that there was 'Jack' on some old letters that were in the bag. He also mentioned my once having had a gun. Its receipt from when I sold it was also in the bag." Dave grunted noncommittally.

"So-- I called Norfolk Police Department." Jack gave no notice of a sharp intake of breath from Dave. "Eventually I got hold of a senior detective sergeant. He listened to my story, then seemed to become quite enthused about the matter when I mentioned the note I had received. He asked whether he could put me on speaker phone to his squad room, so all of his detectives could hear me read the letter. He kept mentioning the possibility of there being 'clues' they could discern. I agreed, and began reading. He interrupted, suggesting that since the note specifically directed the letter be sung, that perhaps I could sing it. Again, I agreed, and proceeded." He shook his head dejectedly. "It was a horrible mistake. I finished singing it, and there was an ominous, overwhelming silence. Then the entire squad room exploded into laughter. They were screeching. Howling. Falling off their chairs. Somebody sounded as though he was getting sick. It was humiliating." He shook his head again. "I was absolutely shocked at their lack of professionalism, and vowed never to speak with them again." Jack's voice quavered indignantly.

Smith and Dave avoided making eye contact with each other, and stonily maintained neutral facial expressions.

"So. I next contacted Naval Intelligence. They dispatched two investigators." He grimaced. "Enlisted men. Senior enlisted, to be fair. But enlisted men, nonetheless. They listened politely, read the letter, and to their credit, did not laugh." Another grimace. "Though I could tell they wanted to. They then asked whether I had preserved the letter and envelope for fingerprints, and when I admitted I had not, they took it into evidence to attach to their report."

Smith carefully cleared his throat, and said, "Too bad you didn't make a copy of it, Jack. It sounds interesting." He paused. "Did the guy threaten you?"

"Not at all. The letter has a taunting tone, and admissions of an addictive life-style, but as it was mailed from Atlanta, I believe the man has since moved and begun life over. Hopefully, the monetary gains he made from my belongings helped give him a fresh start."

"So did you make a copy of the letter, or not?"

"Of course I copied it. I study it on occasion, seeking additional insights." He pulled to a stop in the restaurant's parking lot, and pulled a folded page from his jacket pocket. "If you would like, I'll recite it for you." He turned on the dome light, and began:

"A Chrismas Carol" (Sing it to the tune of "Jingle Bells", asshole)

Life too cool,

You a fool,

I gots all yo' stuff.

Hit the hock,

And scored some rock,

But it ain't near enough.

You park yo' ride,

And I inside,

Before you out of sight.

Stole yo' shit,

And hit the bricks,

And run into the night.

You wish you had yo' gun,

Well I wish you did, too,

You'd leave it in yo' car,

And I take it from you.(hahaha)

Poleece don't chase me,

They do, I just flee,

And you'd say 'Shoot that filthy scrote,

But aim around my coat."

Yo---Christmas time,

Life too fine,

I just smile all day.

Some day, Jack,

When you come back,

I'll steal yo' Chevrolet.

Jack carefully folded the page, and turned in his seat. "Well, guys-- what is your opinion?"

"Jack," said Smith, "I think your assessment is insightful and absolutely flawless." He carefully avoided looking at Dave. "And I agree with your conclusions." Dave nodded somber agreement.

"Well. Good. Very good." He nodded crisply, once, obviously content with his conclusions. "Just as I hoped. Dinner, gentlemen?"

FREAK OF NATURE

By Mike Stamm
(Finalist)

Troopers working daylight shifts usually ride in one-man patrol units. Although that theoretically means that there are twice as many Departmental units in the area to provide back-up, it seldom reflects reality. Day-shift officers are often in court, transporting prisoners, or performing administrative duties that inevitably occur when there is a glut of command-type, day-shift, flat-assed, desk-driving bureaucrats on duty who see troopers as time-saving personal servants. Or so it often seems, to the road troops.

A trooper working nights has his back-up partner riding with him, while a lone daylight-hours troop must wait for requested back-up units to arrive, assuming he has time to call for help. Troopers waiting for assistance are reminded of a fact that all children seem to instinctively note— that while time might fly while you're having fun, a few moments of misery can seem interminable.

Resourceful officers use everything possible to their advantage— lighting, cover, terrain, surprise, distraction, to name just a few. They're also not shy about calling upon unconventional sources to protect themselves. Such help can come in the form of a sympathetic witness, an unexpected source of information, or a citizen eager to help. Each of those sources have saved countless troopers from injury or death along the state's highways.

When the threat to the trooper is an entrenched bureaucracy, more serious sources of aid must be enlisted...

"I had a citizen come into the post today, to personally discuss his contact with you last week, Smith," the lieutenant said tiredly from behind his desk.

Smith, mimicking his post commander's apparent exhaustion, shook his head in amazement.

"Tenente, I am shocked and taken aback. I just don't know what this world is coming to." He exhaled loudly, rubbed a wide hand across his face and said, "Citizens are unappreciative, miserable malcontents, sir, every damned one of 'em, and we both know you can't believe a word they say." He pursed his lips in disgust. "What total fabrications did this cretin burden you with, sir?"

The lieutenant scooped a complaint report toward Smith, with his own notes attached. "It involved your arrest of a drunk driver early Sunday afternoon."

"Sunday?" Smith gave all indications of trying to recall blurred events from the distant past. "Sunday?" he repeated. "A drunk driver, you said?"

"Smith, goddmamnit," the lieutenant exploded. "Don't dance me around. I believe you might forget what days you're supposed to come to work, and I wouldn't be surprised if you've forgotten your own birthday, but I know for a fact that you remember every person you've ever arrested."

Smith's vague expression remained fixed, and he pulled dully at his lower lip. "Herr Leutnant," he said, "you're gonna have to help me out, here." He shrugged widely, "I'm drawing a blank. Who did I arrest for OUIL last Sunday who might conceivably have a complaint?"

It was the lieutenant's turn to scrub palms across his face in exhaustion. *Both hands,* noted Smith, *when you use both hands, you look much more tired. I gotta remember that.*

"Bean. Dan Bean, from Oklahoma," said the lieutenant, sharply. "Ring any bells, Smith?"

"Oh. Sure El-Tee. I remember now. And 'ringing bells' is a more appropriate a term than you might imagine. But that complaint is under a different file class than OUIL. He got arrested for Assaulting a Police Officer, Resisting and Obstructing a Police Officer-- specifically, our own beloved Trooper Smith-- Open Intoxicants in a Motor Vehicle, and Possession of Marijuana. And," he conceded, "OUIL. So," Smith asked, leaning forward eagerly, "just what did that overgrown, sad-sack, gravel-faced, leg-humper have to complain about today?"

"I didn't talk to Mister Bean," sniffed the lieutenant. "Although the sergeant who was on duty that day mentioned that Bean *did* have gravel embedded in his face at the time of his arrest."

"Well," drawled Smith, "I hate to split hairs, but at the time he was arrested, Bean looked just fine. It was after he resisted that arrest and assaulted me that he picked up the load of gravel." He ignored the lieutenant's dismissive wave, and continued, "So. The lummox came in to complain he got his ass handed to him by a troop half his size?" He snorted in disgust. "He ought to be ashamed of himself."

"Bean didn't make a complaint. A witness came in to talk to me."

"One of his friends? They got no complaints, they were both bigger than me, too! Besides, I offered them a chance to fight when he and I got done," he declared indignantly. "They both made it clear that they'd seen enough, when their buddy Bean got beaned." Smith chuckled modestly at his own joke, "And they said they didn't want to catch an ass-kicking, too." He grinned and added, "Here's exactly what one of them said," he said, joyously offering an imitation. Smith rubbed his jaw reflectively, scrutinized an object at floor level, and in his best version of an Oklahoma accent said, "Ah ain't got no dawg in thay-at damn' fight."

The lieutenant seemed unmoved by the impression.

"Neither of the passengers complained," the lieutenant said. "Yet," he added pointedly. "I heard from the complainant-- the owner of a welding shop who called in the drunk-driver report from his car."

"Mister Johnson?" exclaimed Smith. "Why didn't you say so? Now, there's a credible witness, Lukanela; that guy is salt of the earth. Whatever he says I did wrong, I by-God did wrong. What did he complain about? Probably that hat thing again. I swear, I had a feeling there was going to be one hell of a donnybrook, so I left the hat on my back seat for safekeeping. And when it came time to sort the pepper from the fly shit, it turns out to have been a wise choice," he insisted, "what with me being attacked, and all. You know how I treasure that hat, sir."

"We're not here to talk about your hat, Smith."

"Of course not," Smith looked somber. "Refresh my memory, sir. Just what the hell *are* we here for?"

"Mr. Johnson wanted me to know what took place. He said that after calling in a report of a drunk driver, he kept him in sight until you stopped the suspect vehicle, then stopped to offer assistance if you needed it. He gave me a royal chewing-out for sitting inside on my fat ass while sending one trooper to stop three huge drunks, incidentally. He said that's how troopers get killed, and that if he ran his welding shop that way, he'd be out of business." The lieutenant paused, composing himself.

"So. Did you apologize to the citizen, and promise to start working for a living?"

Smith was met with an icy glare.

"I didn't really expect to see your name on today's patrol schedule," Smith said sullenly.

"Mr. Johnson said you spoke calmly and politely to Bean, though he admitted he couldn't hear the words. He said that upon failing several roadside sobriety tests, Bean became visibly agitated."

"Couldn't have phrased it better myself, sir."

"What was said?"

"Well, sir, I told Mr. Bean he was under arrest, and he told me he wasn't. He then said he was getting back into his car, and I said he wasn't. Then Bean said he was going to kick my ass." Smith seemed content to end the story there.

"And…" coaxed the lieutenant.

"And-- I said he probably could, but that he was way too big for me to fight with."

"Too big? What is this guy's physical?"

"His Oklahoma operator's license said he was six feet, eight inches tall, and that he weighed 285 pounds. Personally, I believe the State of Oklahoma and old Dan are both prone to understatement."

"So, what exactly did you say to him, Smith?"

"I said, 'Dan, I'm not gonna fight with you. You're just too damned big. You know,' I said, 'in my family I'm considered to be kind of a runt, but you'd be big even if you were one of my cousins.' I said, 'Look at you, Dan-- you're a freak of nature. You're tall enough to eat an apple off the top of my head.' "

"You called him 'a freak of nature'? Is that when he attacked you?"

"No, sir. He took that right in stride, knowing I meant it in the most positive sense. In fact, he calmed down for a few moments, until I had the two passengers and their dog get out of the Blazer, and I started to search the vehicle interior."

"Why didn't you wait for back-up?"

Smith shrugged. "I couldn't wait to stop him, Lefteanant, or he'd've hit somebody. Back-up was going to get there when it got there, so I figured I'd toss the vehicle and yank its keys while I was waiting." Another shrug.

"Let's get to the assault. What happened?"

"Well, sir, it's like I said in the report. Bean was running hot-and-cold, as drunks often do. He decided he was leaving, and came around to the door of his vehicle and ordered me to get out of his way. I tried to reason with him, but he wouldn't have it. So, I told him he was under arrest for OUIL. He seemed completely underwhelmed, so I told him that if he didn't submit to handcuffing, I'd be forced to charge him with Resisting

Arrest. That's when he said he'd had all the arresting he was going to tolerate, and reached over and grabbed me by the upper arm, and picked me off the ground like I was a child."

"How far away was your back-up at that point?"

"I'd have to guess it was somewhere on the far side of the moon, sir. It didn't show until the dust had settled. In any event, when Bean set me down I shook my upper arm loose," Smith demonstrated, "and gave him my angriest glare." Smith contorted his face accordingly. "He glared right back at me. And then-- well, sir-- and then, I just smiled at him."

"You what?" boomed the lieutenant, pawing through the report with one hand to find mention of this tactic, and slurping noisily at his cup of coffee.

"I just smiled, Leitnats," admitted Smith, wistfully. "And, you know, my dear old Mother was right. 'Smile, and the world smiles with you', she always says. I smiled bright as day and for one golden moment, Bean forgot how intent he was upon leaving, and how upset he was about my placing him under arrest, and he even forgot how perturbed I had gotten about being manhandled and assaulted. And that big old goof just stood there smiling back at me." Smith's smile disappeared. "And then," he said flatly, "I kicked him in the balls."

The lieutenant coughed violently, spraying coffee in a dark cloud across his desk.

"Bless you, sir. And Citizen Daniel Bean," he continued calmly, "who just a few minutes before had thought that his life was progressing rather smoothly, suddenly came to the realization that we were taking our little discussion to a whole new level. He made a deep, soggy, croaking sound-- it was truly ugly, sir-- and clutched at himself with one hand. The other hand came at my head like a catcher's mitt, and I knew if he grabbed onto me I'd have to shoot him. So, I snagged his thumb with one hand, and his little finger-- which was none too little, by the way-- with my other hand, and I twisted him off-balance and spun him down the bank like I was rolling a barrel. He ended up flat on his chest, but pushed himself up off the ground with one hand. I was on his back at the time, so I thought he might be getting his wind back. I reefed his wrist up behind his ear, and swore to Great God Almighty I'd twist Bean's arm off and beat his ugly head in with it unless he let me get my arresting done. He agreed to my handcuffing him, then I dragged him up the bank and slammed him in the back seat. I brushed my hands off, turned to the two passengers, and said, 'C'mon, damn it. I can whip you both, and your ugly damned hound, too.' But I guess I already told you what they did." Smith tipped his palms upward. "And that, Hadnagy, was that."

The lieutenant sat, wordlessly shaking his head, then asked, "You kicked him in the balls?"

"Yes, sir, I most certainly did." Still another shrug. "It's a little trick a partner showed me once, and it just seemed like the thing to do at the time."

"How hard did you kick him?"

Smith pondered before answering. "I'd have to say I did it with considerable enthusiasm, sir. As a general rule, I've found that kicking big angry drunks in the balls is one of those activities you want to get right the first time."

"The witness said you pulled some fancy kung-fu move on the suspect," said the lieutenant accusingly. "This karate move was just a kick in the balls?" He massaged his eyes with his fingertips and slumped further into his chair before repeating, "How hard did you kick him?"

"I'm glad you asked again, sir. I kicked the crease right out of a pair of freshly-pressed uniform pants-- one leg of them, anyway. I kicked him so hard I could feel his testicles slap together through the sole of my boot. Why, I ..."

"Enough, Smith."

"Hard, sir. Damned awful hard."

"I said that's enough, Smith."

"Yessir." Smith drew a breath, and brightly resumed. "So, what exactly was Mr. Johnson's complaint, anyway?"

The lieutenant exhaustedly pulled himself upright in his chair.

"Johnson had no complaint, other than you being sent out alone to deal with a carload of dangerous drunks. He said that he wanted me to put you in for the Medal of Honor." The lieutenant sorrowfully surveyed at his coffee-sprayed desktop. "Get the hell out of here, Smith."

"Absolutely," Smith stood and turned toward the door, then paused. "So. Does this mean I don't get the Medal of Honor?"

"We don't have a Medal of Honor, Smith. You know that."

"I'd be happy to accept any MSP equivalent, Obersturmfuhrer; Valor, Bravery. Heck, even a Meritorious would be better than nothing."

"You don't wear the last medal we gave you, Smith."

"I don't wear my hat very often, either, but I just got done telling you how much it means to me."

"What is it with you, Smith?" the lieutenant demanded with sudden vehemence. "Most troops can hardly wait to put any decorations they're awarded on their uniforms.

Yours sit around drawing dust somewhere."

"Orders don't say you have to wear them, Loo."

"It's assumed you'd want to wear them. I've been in this department for thirty years, and I've never received a decoration."

"If you were to give me a Medal of Honor, I'd let you borrow mine, buddy."

"You're not getting a goddamned Medal of Honor, Smith. And I'm not your buddy."

"I suspected as much when you thwarted my being awarded the Medal of Honor," said Smith, archly. He opened the office door, then turned again, his archness apparently forgotten. "You know, sir, whenever citizens bitch about me, it always gets put on paper and jammed into my files." He failed to wilt under the lieutenant's glare, and continued. "It just seems like an attaboy would be put into my file too, particularly considering how rare an event it is. Especially since I'm getting screwed out of my Kung-Fu Street Fighter Medal of Honor."

The lieutenant gave another ragged exhalation. "There will be a letter of citizen praise put in your personnel files, Smith. Now-- for the love of Christ-- please, get out of my office."

Smith gave the lieutenant the same smile he had shared with Mr. Bean and left, closing the office door behind him.

"Is our car loaded, partner?" he asked O'Brian.

"Sure. You OK?"

"Right as rain." He raised index finger and thumb a hair's-breadth apart. "You might not believe this, Obee, but I came *this close* to being awarded the Medal of Honor today," he boasted.

"You don't wear the last medals they gave you."

"You're not the first person to point that out today," admitted Smith, settling into their unit. "God, I love this job!" he exclaimed.

Obie pulled from the post parking lot and looked sidelong at Smith.

"Good thing the District secretary gave you a heads-up on that citizen coming in today, huh?"

"Absolutely. If Miz Rhonda doesn't know about it, it isn't worth knowing, I always say."

"She always gives you a call when you're being checked out by the brass."

"She does. Rhonda and I are buddies." Smith hooked a thumb over his shoulder, toward the post. "Some folks at that place don't want to be my buddy, but I'm mature enough to accept that," he said pointedly. "But Miz Rhonda and I are buddies from way back, and I always use her warnings to prepare to defend myself from unjust oppression. If she hadn't called my house and talked with my wife this morning, I never would have taken the time to learn how to say 'lieutenant' in several languages."

"I'm impressed, and I'm betting the lieutenant is delighted with your efforts. It's attention to details that gets you ahead in this outfit. How is the Old Man, today?"

"Showing his age, I fear. Poor old guy can't even make it through a cup of coffee without spilling it all over himself." He nodded sadly. "I do my best to keep his spirits up but I swear, some days he seems to age before my very eyes.

Aldo and The Giant
The Christmas Carol
Freak of Nature

About the Author

My name is Mike Stamm. I am a former Michigan State Police trooper, honorably retired with a duty-incurred physical disability after sixteen years' service. Assigned to Uniform Division, served at Bay City, Bridgeport (Saginaw area), Detroit Freeway, and Paw Paw posts. My current activities include private-sector firearms instructor, private investigator (licensed in Michigan, Indiana, Illinois, Ohio, and Wisconsin), and assistant projectionist at the Strand Theater, Paw Paw, MI.

My wife of nearly 30 years and I live in a 155-year-old farmhouse on 33 acres, upon which I hunt, plant trees, and wander aimlessly with my hounds.

My American Heroes: The warriors of HMLS 302

By Robert P. Mueck
(Finalist)

I was waiting for them when they arrived – all of them on their own two feet. Several of them walked with a limp. Some used crutches, some used canes, and some had no ailments visible to the naked eye. They were students in my class, but these men would show me that I was the student. Let me explain.

I am an adjunct Professor for the University of Maryland University College (UMUC) and I teach an undergraduate class in Homeland Security. After 23 years as a police officer with time in the Army and Coast Guard Reserve, I was finally doing something for my life after retirement – teaching. For my fall 2008 class, I was asked to teach at the Walter Reed Army Medical Center (WRAMC) in Washington DC. It wasn't exactly on my way home or to work, but I thought it would be nice to contribute to these warriors as they transitioned out of the military. Little did I know what an impact the class would have on me.

I went to WRAMC two weeks before the class was to start to make sure I knew where the classroom was and to get access to the Army Education Center where I would be teaching. On that day, I met a young soldier who wanted to sign up for the class. He was in a wheel chair – his left leg missing at the knee, his left arm missing at the elbow, his left ear gone, the left side of his face scarred. I barely knew what to say. All I could blurt out was, "How are you doing?" He nodded his head and told me that some days are better than others, but 'today' was a good day. I told him that he needed to focus on the good days and he'd be all right. I remember thinking to myself that this was going to be a tough semester.

On the first day of class, I arrived early. I had my PowerPoint presentation set up and qued up the computer for the DVD. I had rehearsed my introduction, made copies of the syllabus, and prepared for this class to get the semester going. Twenty four students were registered for the class. Four of them were UMUC students who happened to register for this class. Several of them were members of the military who are working on their college degrees. And several of them were wounded warriors – soldiers who had been injured in combat and were being treated and transitioning out of the Army. All of them happened to be male – purely by chance. This was that day I was waiting for them when they arrived. These are the men who are my American Heroes.

For their own privacy, I won't name them, other than to mention their first names. But the men I now hold as my heroes were the students in my class. Where do I begin? The young soldier in the wheelchair didn't make it to class and had to drop his enrollment. But I got to know the rest of the class over the course of the semester.

There was Johnnie from Tennessee. His family has participated in every war ever fought by this country except for the Gulf war. Johnnie had served in the Army when Reagan was President, but he decided he couldn't let the legacy of his family service end with him. So sixteen years after he left the Army, he re-enlisted and volunteered for service in Iraq. He was wounded there driving a heavy transport vehicle. An IED took out his truck and he survived the explosion. While undergoing treatment for his injury, Army doctors found he had blocked arteries and required a heart bypass. Imagine - his combat injury actually saved his life. Had he not been wounded, there is a good chance that his blocked arteries would not have been discovered. He is recovering and will be allowed to remain in the Army. For him, his injury saved his life. His next stop, if he can get it, is Afghanistan...after he gets married. Johnnie was slated to be home for Christmas, but his plans were scrapped. The Army found a knee problem and promptly scheduled him for surgery. Once that is done, he's due for a hernia operation. Johnny won't be going home until later in

2009. As he said, he'll look like a carved Turkey, but at least everything will be working.

There was Shawn, the soldier from Colorado who has a scar from his right eye, over his scalp, to the behind his right ear. He too was caught in an IED, and suffers from a concussive brain injury that makes it hard for him to concentrate at times. Occasionally he would have a hard time asking a question – he had a hard time phrasing it properly, or he'd ask the same question twice. He felt self-conscious about it, but no one would ever say anything about it. He was accepted for whom he is, and he did well in the class. His wife and daughters are waiting for him in Germany, so once he is out of the Army, he'll be returning to them. For him, his Army career has come to an end.

There was the young soldier named Geraldo who pulled me aside one day to ask about qualifications to be a police officer. He's from New Jersey and he suffered an injury in Iraq where his Achilles tendon was blown out. He is awaiting a cadaver tendon and doctors have told him that he'll be as good as new once everything is done. He wants to return to New Jersey and become a cop in his home town. Geraldo has been involved in a few fire fights with the 10th Mountain Division and he's ready to get out. He is a great candidate for a police career, except that he's not old enough (at least not in Maryland)! This year he will qualify when he turns 21, but he's not there yet. Of course, he has more experience in a fire fight than my entire police department combined. New Jersey – get ready. You have one sharp guy coming your way in public service.

There was also the other young soldier from New Jersey, Ryan, also the victim of an IED, who also suffers from a concussive brain injury. He is quick with his comments and occasionally talked a bit loud, but he was respectful, always raised his hand, and worked hard on his studies. While being treated, it was discovered that he suffers Crohns' disease, so he is now going through treatment for that ailment. He considered quitting the class to focus on getting healthy, but he made it and passed with flying colors. He joined the Army after 9/11 and is being transitioned out of the military. A new life awaits him as he makes his way out of the Army.

Then there was an older soldier named Dewitt from the DC National Guard. He came to class one day with his ears full of piercings. It turns out that they were not any kind of fashion statement. Rather, they were part of an acupuncture treatment to reduce the pain in his back. He said they worked, though God only knows how. He's a local to the DC area, but he survived several IED explosions and he's happy to be home. He wears the patch of the 82nd Airborne on the combat side of his uniform. He didn't talk much about himself, but it was clear that he suffered from pain on a regular basis and is on the mend.

There was another Army guy, a Senior NCO, by the name of Tim. Tim is a tough guy, street smart and opinionated. But occasionally one would glimpse the soft side of him. While he recovers from his injuries he walks with a cane. Some days he seemed okay, other days he looked years older. Sometimes he would be a bit late, but he always made it to class. What stood out from him was that he would ask ME how I was doing? "Me? Hell, I'm fine...how about you?" "Doing okay." When a class discussion got a bit off target or loud, Tim would bring it back on track for me, or quiet it down. He played the role of the enforcer and would allow the class to stay on task. The Army is going to lose a good man when he gets out.

There was also the Army guy who was very quiet. He would contribute on occasion, and when he did, his comments always contributed value to the topic being discussed. Ed, I later learned, is a First Sergeant (1SG) with 29 years in the Army. He was hoping to make it to 30 years, but that may be cut short as he transitions out due to his injuries.

Then there was Darrell, who also walked with a cane. Darrel is a young guy who was looking forward to his time in the Army. His injury cut that short, and now he is looking at returning to civilian life. I asked Darrell how his leg was doing, and he told me that it is about as good as it is going to get. He has no feeling in his foot, so it is hard to control how he walks at times. He's in pain a lot and he won't be able to run anymore...but he has his foot and can walk. It could have been worse.

I could go on. There are the two Army guys who aren't wounded. They are stationed at Walter Reed and are taking college classes to help them in the future. There are the two Navy guys who make the drive within the DC area to attend class. One of them, Rey, is very quiet but extremely attentive and very bright. The other one, Atekwana, is an immigrant from Africa who serves proudly in the Navy.

So, how are these men my heroes? It's not the injuries that make them my heroes, though that is a part of it. It's simply that they served in the front lines and continue to serve. Some of them survived their injuries and are working on rebuilding their lives. They are living in pain, enduring physical therapy or surgery, and continuing to attend college classes to brighten their futures. They willingly served and some of them are staying in the army because they choose to do so. They want to make a difference is some way and now that they are wounded they are taking the time to get a higher education while recovering.

How very lucky we are to have these men among us. How very lucky I was to be a part of this class. I used to belong to the American Society of Law Enforcement Trainers (ASLET) whose motto was "Those that Teach, Learn." Never has that motto rung more true than in the fall of 2008. These men inspired me and reminded me of what an honor it was to be a part of that class. As I watched and listened and talked to them, I found solace in their individual struggles. Not that I was happy to see them struggle, but that they stood up to their struggles to put their lives back together again. They didn't give up. They got hurt fighting and continue to fight. And they aren't done. They took a class in Homeland Security because they hope to keep a place in public service. They want to stay in the fight against terrorism – for some, the very reason they joined the military. Knowing that, I realized that our country is going to be okay. We talk about the greatest generation as if there are no longer any such people around. But they are...I know... I met them... In HMLS 302. They taught me a new respect for life, and for that I am indebted to them. I may have taught the class, but in another sense, I was the student.

My American Heroes:
The warriors of HMLS 302

About the Author

Robert Mueck is a Lieutenant with the University of Maryland Police in College Park. He is also an adjunct faculty member at the University of Maryland University College where he teaches a class in Homeland Security. Bob has been a cop for 23 years, working in patrol, investigations, administrative jobs, and operations. He is currently the commander of the SERT team, a street-crimes unit. Bob is a veteran of the US Army and US Coast Guard Reserve, and is proud to be an Army Brat. He is married with four children and lives in the State of Maryland.

Behind the Badge

By Susan Tutko

I'm writing this so that my feelings are down on black and white of how my life has Changed in so many ways since *my husband became a police officer.*

Not really sure were I should start, I guess the beginning would be good.

Let's see, many years my husband was in the medical field, he has his doctorate and his PHD.

He worked very hard to receive them.

Mind you before he got all that, he was working at all different kinds of places but Was never really happy.

He worked in hospitals, clinics doctors offices, he said he was happy and I believed him.

But there was something missing and I couldn't put my finger on it.

Know matter what kind of job he did he worked hard and put over 100% into it.

Since he was in high school he always wanted to be a police officer whether it was to take after his uncle who also was his Godfather, a man he looked up to. But what ever the reason was, he never put it out of his mind.

His parents said "no" I said "no." With two little ones I wasn't going to have it, the worries and the long nights and what ever else came along with that. No, this wasn't the time for a job change after all these years in the medical field.

I think I was more afraid of what I didn't know of the job more than I didn't think he could handle it because he could handle anything that was in front of him.

Until one day he said to me "Look Sue. Look at this" as he pointed to the newspaper.

It was an ad that the Memphis Police Department was hiring. I was like "ah no sir." He said, Come on. Let me apply and see what happens."

At this time my girls were in high school and in my head I thought, ok if he gets in its ok, the girls are not little anymore. It will be ok.

But how were my girls going to handle it? They informed me that they couldn't see their dad wearing a police uniform; they only knew him wearing his hospital whites.

They had their own fears and feelings on this and again, I think it was that they to were not certain of what the job was all about and just wanted their Dad to be Dad wearing the whites as they knew him.

I thought about it for awhile and said, "Ok go ahead and apply and see what happens.

He also applied for the a position in a different city and they didn't hire him because they told him he was too smart, Ah! Ok. They also stated he wouldn't last that long with that department ,he would move on if he saw a better opportunity. Hmm makes me wonder, who do they hire ? Well, its their loss.

He got on with Shelby County Sheriffs Department, volunteer of course but in his training he blew out his knee and missed too many days. If he wanted to go back, he had to start all over again, he wasn't having that.

Well lo and behold, the Memphis Police Department contacted him and informed him that he had to go through more red tape of background checks and what have you and once all was done, he was finally informed he could start the police academy.

Mind you, just because he got into the academy he wasn't safe because he needed to pass tests after test and the physical exercise training. If he didn't he was out, meaning he couldn't become a officer. Now we both knew he was book smart, so we knew he would pass that with flying colors.

He is a team player and is willing to help anyone. But when it came to the physical exercise, this is where it got interesting. The two mile run for him felt like 10 miles.

At the end of the day he would actually roll out of the car exhausted feeling like he got run over by an 18 wheeler truck. As well as getting the "wall" as he puts it. That was tough as well. It took all the energy he had left just to take his clothes off and get into a hot tub.

Every day he would say… "I don't know how much more I can take. It's getting harder and harder." But in the same breath he would say, "I'm not giving up."

All his hard work paid off. He graduated on a cold winter night December 10, 1998. As he stood there in his uniform without his badge pinned on, alongside his colleges, he looked different to me. He looked stronger and he was so proud of what he accomplished.

As I looked around the room, looking at others who were about to get their badge pinned on after they approached the stage, the looks on the faces were of uncertain.

The faces of the new police officers that would enforce our streets looked like "I finally made it and some faces looked like they couldn't believe it was over and they would actually have to wear a gun and badge; the look of "Am I ready for this?"

I looked at my husband's mother and father and his father had this glowing look about him and a tear came off his cheek. He was so proud of his son as if he took his first step or spoke his first word, another milestone his son had achieved and he was proud to be his Dad that day. His Mom was smiling from ear to ear. Her son was to become a cop and she too was proud of him. Our girls were very happy for their dad and proud of what he has done and achieved.

As for me, wow! This was overwhelming for me. All these men and women in blue; what they must be thinking what is going on in their heads? I looked over to my husband and he was standing just so tall and proud. I was proud of him for all his hard work and all that he went through to get to where he was today. Go figure? My husband was going to be a cop.

Once the badge was pinned on him and everyone else, we tried to find each other in the crowd. It was like a movie and slow motion. We couldn't reach each other. We saw each other but couldn't get to one another. Then, all of a sudden, there was a opening in the crowd and there we stood, looking each other as others moved around us.

He grabbed my hand and pulled me toward him and kissed me and hugged me oh so tight. He told me he loved me as I told him I loved him as well. This hug was different than all the other hugs he had ever given me.

At the moment, I realized his life was about to change and so was mine. I have to get used to a gun in the house and my husband wearing a badge, along with him carrying a gun. Wow! Already my life had changed.

I wasn't worried about him; not one bit, because I knew he could take care of himself and how strong of a person he was. Or was I worried and didn't want to show it?

I was asked one day if I had any regrets about him being a cop? I took a bit to answer and then I said "yes," they looked at me and tilted their heads a bit and said "really," I said "yes, only one regret. I regret that he didn't do this earlier in his life because I have never seen him happier. This is his dream come true and I'm not going to stand between that."

His first tour of duty was he needed to be Santa Claus at the local school. Talk about the spirit of Christmas... Now Santa carries a gun under his suit.

Within a short period of time we got word that an officer had died in the line of duty. We had never experienced this before so we did not know what to expect.

When a officer dies in the line of duty, I believe all of the officers, male and female, feel like a piece has been taken from them. The bond of police officers and the brotherhood is so strong between them it is as if they become one.

My husband put on his dress blues and I got into my Sunday best and we headed to the Funeral parlor.

I was over whelmed when we got close to the parlor. Cars everywhere and people all around. We went into the parlor to pay our respects to the officer's family and as I walked, I saw grown men crying, men wiping their faces from tears,hugging and telling each other how sorry they are. My heart skipped a beat as we waited in line.

I thought to myself, "dear Lord, I do not ever want to have to go though this. This was the saddest thing I have ever been though."

Once it was our turn to speak to the family, I became speechless. When I approached his wife, she was pregnant and looked so lost and hurt, I just saw myself standing there for a moment and froze. I got a grip and moved toward her and I just lost it. I told her I was so sorry for her loss and that I would pray for her and her family. Are those the right words to say? I don't know. I just don't know.

All I know is we lost a good man, a person who protected us from crime, someone's husband, son, and soon to be father. He was gone and it was hard to handle.

As I walked up to the coffin, I saw the officer in his uniform laying there and I kneeled down to pray for his soul. I looked up at the uniform he was wearing and saw these medals and this man laying there, and as I turned to look at his wife, I could just feel her pain. It was horrible.

We left and my husband held my hand and said nothing to me as we both wiped our tears from our faces. It was as if we both knew how we felt and words were not needed.

From that day I realized that I could not just think he went to a job and would be home at the end of the day because, as we saw, things happen and we just can't see the future.

I look forward to his call when he says he is on his way home and to see him come into the house at the end of his tour. It lifts my heart and feels good to know he is home safe. Especially when he has a day off. It's like a breather for me. I don't have to worry about it because I know were he is and what he is doing. Again, my life has changed.

A few months passed by and another officer died in the line of duty. Oh no. Not again. This can't be happening. This is not supposed to happen like this. Not so soon. Not at all. Once again, the dress blues go on and we go to pay our respects. Again the whole place is filled with officers paying their respects.

Again the tears from these men who go out everyday to serve and protect us. These strong men who act like superman. They are crying, standing in shock and numb.

Well let me tell you a secret. They are not superman. They are human as you and I. They cry and hurt and bleed like everyone else. Just because you put a vest and uniform on them and they carry a gun doesn't' make them inhuman; they still have feelings.

I have no idea what my husband is thinking but I can sure see how he feels. He is hurt and sad and there are no words in the world at this time that will make him any different.

I once again think about what kind of a job my husband has and how he puts his life on the line for stangers everyday that he leaves the house and how much more I love him for what he does.

I cannot expect my husband to wallow in the filth of society day in and day out without my full support and my prayers. He has a tough job; a very tough job. Who amongst us is willing to give our lives for people we don't know or for people who don't care about them? That is what my husband is willing to do everyday he puts on his uniform and he leaves his home.

My husband was on days for a while then Delta (which we both didn't like) and now he is on Charlie shift; 2-10. It's not a bad shift but let me tell you, its not the best neighborhood to patrol. As a matter of fact, he is in the worst neighborhood in Memphis. I wish he was on days. He says he wants this shift for many reasons, money, position with the union, and seniority. Ok. Ok He knows best, I think, but the worst neighborhood. Come on!

In the beginning I said I didn't worry when he went off to work. Well, my feelings are different now. I watch the clock and wait for him to call to tell me he is on his way home. Why, you ask? Well after the years he has been on the force he has been through a lot more then he is willing to share with me.

I worry about making sure someone is there to back him up. I worry about the bad guy; what he might do. So, yes, I do worry about him now when he goes to work more then he'll ever know.

A police officer's life is full of death and, what most people would call, unusual situations. To remain a Police Officer a person has to learn to deal with the stress and emotional ups and downs. Can you do that? I can honestly say, I can't.

I know that he has seen more then he wishes to share with me because he knows I would be upset. Fights,shootings,familys being torn apart, babies crying, car accidents, blood and death taking people to jail. If someone can do this every day, they have my blessing. My husband he deals with this, so that is why his home should a safe place.

This brings me to a car accident that we saw on our way home from our vacation. Cars were backed up for miles, 5 or 6 police cars with their lights flashing and yellow tape draped across the road and then, there it was; a body in the middle of the street with a sheet over it.I felt sick to my stomach and just was worried about the family who would have to be notified of the loss of their loved one.

It was very sad and very emotional for me. I turned to my husband and he really didn't have the same look I had and by what I could see not even the same feelings I felt. I said, "Honey how can you do this day after day?

I don't get it." He says he detaches himself from it and just does his job. Some may call this heartless, but call it what you will, I figure if he didn't do that, his emotions would overwhelm him and he would lose control of what his job was.

I'm sure you may think that he is cold or cynical to all that is around him but don't think that unless you have walked in his boots as long as he has walked in them and done his job.

Many people who do not work as police officers cannot understand what seeing and dealing with hurt, dead or dying people day after day does to a person. I'm just a wife of a cop and this is just my observation.

He has to deal with the violence in his own way. Often that is done by drawing into himself and opening up to the only folks who understand him.

I know there have been many nights that he came home at the end of his shift and said nothing, and when it was time for bed he would just lie awake and try to get his emotions on an even keel before he could fall asleep.

Again, my life has changed along with his. We have different things to deal with now plus our normal life situations and problems.

Being a cop family is hard. Hard for the officer and the spouse and the children. You both have to have the understanding of each others feelings and to be there for one another. He loves his work he loves his family he is so dedicated to both and, at time, I'm sure he feels like he is pulled in so many different directions.

I want to end this with one last note …Behind the badge, he is a husband, a father, an uncle, and a grandfather as well as a cop. I see him as a man with many hats and many talents.

What do I see when I look at him? I see a smile that melted my heart when we met. I see a wonderful man who falls into a hole but gets up and brushes himself off and goes on as if nothing happened. I see a great cop and I'm proud to be married to him.

He is my American hero.

Behind the Badge

About the Author

My name is Susan Tutko the wife of the officer in this story.

I was born and raised in Western New York, got married to Bob when I was 19.

We have 2 childern, two girls and 3 grand-daughters and another grand-daughter on the way.

I have been married for 31 years.

I have always wanted to tell someone how I felt about being married to a cop and express how challenging it is.

I hope you enjoy this short story and remember being a police officer isn't just another job.

Be safe.

Dangers, Toils, and Snares

By Tim Casey

If you have never heard the Pipes and Drums play Amazing Grace, then you haven't lived. This tune is always played for a line of duty death and on solemn occasions for firefighters. I cry every single time I hear it played, maybe because of the occasion for which it is played, or maybe it's because I am a wretch.

I'm Not A Hero!

Let us get one thing clear right from the start. As a firefighter, I don't consider myself a hero. I might do heroic things, but I pull a paycheck every couple of weeks for that. Don't get me wrong, I'll throw the hero card down when it's to my advantage, if it gets me a drink, a break on the cost of a meal, or laid, then I'm the biggest hero you ever saw. Just like a doctor is paid to examine you when you are sick and prescribe a plan to get you well or like a mechanic is paid to fix your breaks or a plumber is paid to clean your drains. It is a job plain and simple.

I have been a firefighter for more than thirty years and I have seen a lot and done many things as a firefighter, and I would not describe a single thing I have done as heroic. Have I saved lives? Yes, more than I can count. Have I run into burning buildings when everyone else was running away? Sure, and I was glad those big pants we wear covered the stain from the pee running down my leg. I have had guns shoved in my belly, large pieces of buildings fall on me, and had people swing bats and knives at my head.

Nevertheless, it's not as if I'm forced to do it, I picked this path, and have loved every minute of it. Society, for some reason, has always had a perception that firefighters are heroes, but man, after September 11, 2001, firefighters became golden, but I didn't do anything different on nine eleven than any other day at the firehouse, I watched on TV like everyone else. Maybe I cried a little more than some. However, I didn't cry at the station, I was working that morning when the planes hit. I sat there in silence, me and three other open-mouthed men.

I knew that FDNY had people in those buildings. I knew that they were trying; that's what firefighters do, they find a way. So when the buildings began to fall, I knew that hundreds of firefighters were in there, that they were being crushed like pepper in a grinder, and I knew there were wives, friends, children, moms and dads all over New York who's hearts were dropping just like the towers.

Ever Since 9/11.

I didn't cry there at work, I cried in my car on the way home. There's no crying in fire stations. It's just not done. So I sat at the curb on the side of the road a block from the fire station and bawled my eyes out until I could drive. Then went home and turned the TV on again. FDNY lost more firefighters on that day than worked for my whole department. Just like that, they were gone, and then somehow I became an even bigger hero. I didn't do a damn thing other than cry in my car that day, and now I got people at the gym, that know I'm a firefighter coming up to me and thanking me. Crying in front of me and telling me how much they admire me. One woman who always was standoffish when I tried to chat with her, just started bawling when she saw me the next day at the gym, all she could muster was a weak "Thank you".

What Is It With Women And Firefighters?

The day before I was just that firefighter that works out in their gym, now they're crying in front of me, wanting to hug me and touch me. The check out girl at the grocery store wants to tell me how much she respects what I do. Last week she was as cold as a fish when I was flirting with her, now she respects me. "Really, you do?" "Wanna go out for a drink?" Oh you do (like I said if it gets you laid), how about tonight? If you were a firefighter and couldn't get laid after nine one one, then you either had some serious hygiene problems or you had a wife.

So I hooked up with the checkout girl for a few a dates, then it became strange, I think I can understand how a model feels when men fantasize about them. I was a prop a fantasy thing, it wasn't about me; It was about what I was. She wanted me to bring my firefighting gear to her house and "rescue" her. I'm up for fun and games no harm there, it just ran its course quickly.

Somehow, that day rubbed off on every swinging dick with a blue shirt and a badge, deserved or not. Why? Because we are heroes. Okay, let me also make this clear, if you die in the line of duty, you're a Goddamn hero in my book. On that day, 343 heroes ascended to God's kingdom (as well as 2801 other souls at the World Trade Center). But I didn't deserve any recognition for their act. I was almost the same guy the day after that I was the day before. Was I more aware that my job holds risks? Maybe. Was I worried I was next? No. Every day I suit up could be the last, but it could be the last day at work for all kinds of people. Firefighting doesn't even rank in the top ten most dangerous professions any more. Hell, it's more dangerous to be a fisherman, a farmer, a trucker, or even a construction laborer. Do people hug the guy that grows their asparagus, or the guy that delivers their copy paper? I think not. But I get a hug or even get laid because of the way I make a living. Doesn't seem fair to those other people, does it? You wanna hug a hero? Find a kid in a military uniform that just got back from Iraq and hug him or her. But not me.

So you may ask why I don't consider myself a hero. I tell you why. Because it's my job. A hero, at least in my opinion, does it for free (other than the military). The man or woman that sees a house on fire and runs in and gets people out before I get there, that's heroic. The person that steps in to help a stranger that is hurt or having a heart attack? That's heroic. The people that stop at car wrecks and give aid are heroes. Why? Because they don't have the training I do, they don't wear hundreds of dollars worth of protective clothing like I do. They take a chance and don't get a dime for it, or even know what kind of risks they are taking sometimes. They just help.

I have received hundreds of hours of training to do my job. I have a crew of like trained firefighters at my side at all times. Safety is paramount for us, we generally don't take chances, and when we do, it's a calculated chance, and most of the time those chances come with discipline. Because being unsafe when doing our job is not tolerated by the guys with gold badges. So if you want to hug a hero, the next time you are watching TV and see a toothless dude in a wife beater talking about how he saved his neighbors from their trailer fire, find him and give him a hug.

I Don't Argue With Kids.

Then I get people that want to argue with me about my heroism. They have decided I'm a hero and that is that. So most of the time I just shut up, and agree in a mild way. Because part of me knows that society needs heroes and one huge segment of society that desperately needs heroes are its children. There is no greater single thrill in the entire firefighting profession, in my humble opinion, than sitting on a fire truck motoring down the road and gazing in to a nearby car and seeing a kid light up. They spot you, sometimes they've been staring at you for a few blocks before they catch your eye, and then. Its Christmas morning for a few seconds. Their little eyes just pop out of their heads and they wave like they've been in a lifeboat for a week and you're flying the rescue plane. They just go nuts. I love that moment.

You wave back and if I was stopped at a traffic light, I'd jump off the truck and hand the kid a sticker badge through the window, and if mom was hot of course, she got a badge too. I'll wear the hero moniker for kids, because they deserve to have a hero. With kids you just get to be a hero, there is no definition for them. You wear the hat and the coat and boots, you're a hero. Adults need or want a definition, they have to define your heroism, and you are a hero because... Kids, you got the gear, you're a hero.

One of my favorite memories is of a three-alarm fire years ago. Early one morning just before sunrise, a local restaurant caught fire. It was located in an old train depot right on the tracks. Across the street from the restaurant was a little park that had some old trains on display. My company responded on the second alarm and we were assigned to make an interior attack on the fire. My wife at that time was a firefighter also and she was pregnant with our second child, she had come down to the fire with our son who was three at the time.

As I came out of the burning building, I spotted them on the curb across the street right next to one of the display trains. My son spied me at the same moment and began to wave at me franticly.

Now here I am in all my gear, covered in debris, steam rising off my shoulders and my little boy just glowing at the site of his father the firefighter. My chest puffed out with pride and I squared my shoulders as I walked over to them.

He became more excited the closer I got and began to yell "Dad, dad". So when I reached them I knew I was the biggest hero my kid had ever seen. It was straight out of the movies, a memory locked forever in my mind and his. And then he said something I will never forget as long as I live. He said "Dad did you see the trains?" Those damn trains.

It wouldn't be until years later that my son would realize the true value of having a father that was a firefighter. But on that morning all those years ago, I lost out to some old trains, still makes me laugh today. Talk about keeping your ego in check.

Dangers, Toils, and Snares

About The Author

Tim Casey has been a professional firefighter for more than three decades now, and has been a witness to huge changes in the fire service.

During his firefighting career he has also had many off duty jobs. He was a professional stand-up comic for three and a half years. He has written more than thirty screenplays, and sold three of them. He teaches screenwriting at the University of Colorado in Colorado Springs, and has had dozens of bylines in a multitude of publications. He also was the Director of Public Relations for Pikes Peak Hill Climb Race (America's second oldest auto race) for twelve years.

Tim Casey Has also been the Master of Ceremonies for many large awards shows and has appeared on many taped television shows as well as live broadcasts.

LEONARD C. KASSON

By Wayne E. Beyea

Since the Vietnam War, much has been written about "post traumatic stress syndrome." It seems entirely logical to me that survivors of a war that wasn't a war, where men killed each other because of conflicting ideologies, and young Americans – many still in their teens – watched over 50,000 of their comrades killed, would come away emotionally scarred. It stands to reason those same men who risked their lives in a cause their nation's leaders proclaimed was just, then were spit upon and reviled by their countrymen, rather than being hailed as heroes – would be frustrated, bitter and angry. Twice wounded, Marine Corporal Leonard C. Kasson, recipient of the Purple Heart, Bronze Star and Silver Star, for bravery under fire, was no exception, and his bitterness was exacerbated by the constant perceived shattering of strong beliefs that were dear to his heart; a heart which cared strongly for family, friends, animals, and those unfortunates victimized by the scum of society. Lenny was a classic victim of "post traumatic stress syndrome," yet he scoffed at this psychiatric classification and considered himself misunderstood. This guitar playing, outwardly appearing happy go lucky carefree member of a brotherhood known as the New York State Police, seemed to be the persona of emotional stability. In truth, inside Lenny was a cauldron filled with anger and frustration, needing only a small fire, to bring it to a boil. The constantly changing fire heating the cauldron made him an enigma to all who knew and loved him. Yet, all who worked with Lenny recognized that he was an excellent police officer. Lenny loved his profession, loved solving crime and took great satisfaction in helping the victims of crime. Lenny Kasson would often be described as possessing a big heart and caring deeply about children, family, his brothers in gray, and of course, the Marine Corps. During the approximate 10 years that I knew Lenny, he endeared himself to me, and most of his fellow police officers.

I first met Lenny on a warm spring morning in 1975. A handsome young Trooper walked into the Bureau of Criminal Investigation (BCI) office, where I was laboring to compose an arrest report that would be acceptable by my superiors and the District Attorney. Displaying a warm smile, the Trooper approached, extended his hand and introduced himself as Lenny Kasson. Lenny's handshake was firm, his smile sincere and I was immediately impressed by his offer to help the BCI with investigations, whenever he could. I took this ambitious young Trooper at his word and during the next three years, Lenny provided invaluable assistance to our entire squad of investigators, often working many hours of unpaid overtime to complete his task. It was readily apparent that Lenny preferred conducting criminal investigations over road patrol, loved being a part of the state police family and took great pleasure in "locking up scumbags." At around 5'10" and lean, Lenny did not appear physically imposing; however, he was muscular and as a former combat Marine, he was not to be trifled with. He feared nothing and at times fraught with danger, Lenny remained calm and in control. Lenny was the sort of rare police officer who could quickly win the confidence and cooperation of rape victims, children who had been horribly abused, and also – incredibly - disarm dangerous felons and make them like him.

After meeting Trooper Lenny Kasson, I gained promotion and within a short time was supervisor of the BCI unit. I was pleased when Lenny was promoted to Investigator and became a member of our investigative unit. Lenny proved himself to be an ambitious, tenacious investigator and my only concern about him was that he was pushing too hard. He would work until he dropped from exhaustion, then after taking a short rest, he would return and work until he was exhausted again. Of course, this was an era in which members of the BCI received an annual stipend of 7% of their salary in lieu of paid overtime. I had great confidence in this fearless, dedicated investigator and when I needed backup, Lenny immediately came to mind.

In one particularly challenging incident, the perpetrator happened to be a member of the state police who was going through a difficult divorce and had been placed on mental disability leave. The trooper took a hostage, barricaded himself in his home and threatened to kill his hostage, then himself, unless his wife returned to him. This trooper was also an Army veteran of the Vietnam War, and had been diagnosed as suffering from post-traumatic stress syndrome. I immediately called upon Lenny for assistance. After three days of negotiation we secured the hostage's release; however, the distraught trooper remained barricaded and threatened suicide. On the 4th day of negotiation, I was able to gain entry into the home to continue face-to-face negotiation. However, the trooper remained adamant that his wife come back to him or his death would be on her conscious. Catching the trooper off guard, I jumped him and we fought for possession of his gun. Lenny came to my assistance and together we were able to disarm our brother and save his life.

Outwardly, it appeared that Lenny was able to cope with the emotional beast known as post-traumatic stress syndrome; however, the cauldron of emotional instability within, infrequently started to boil and at those times Lenny became an enigma to all who knew and loved him.

Because Lenny respected me and considered me to be the father he had never known, I was able to check the negative emotions that fueled the flames heating the cauldron.

In 1987, I was offered employment in a high paying security position and retired from the New York State Police. In retirement, I maintained in-frequent contact with Lenny and mistakenly believed he was free of the demons that sparked anger and depression. After my retirement, Lenny was promoted to Zone Sergeant, and transferred to a location that was several hundred miles away. I continued to follow Lenny's career and knew that he remained a tireless, unafraid crime fighter. I would learn that Lenny finally came up against a rabid criminal who he could not convince to surrender. In an exchange of gunfire, Lenny was forced to shoot and kill that individual, to save his life and the lives of others.

I was privileged to be invited to speak at Zone Sergeant Lenny Kasson's retirement dinner, which was well attended. Subsequent to the festivity, Lenny and I embraced each other and promised that we would maintain a close relationship. Sadly, our relationship was all too short.

On a clear, crisp autumn evening in 1999, the ever present and simmering emotional cauldron within him, reached a boiling point. State police were called to respond to retired Zone Sergeant - former Investigator, trooper, Marine Corporal, Leonard Kasson's home. A sardonic, diabolic tragedy began to unfold, as the military and state police hero whom I had trained as a hostage negotiator and who had been the protagonist in many confrontations with suicidal and deranged suspects, was now the armed antagonist in a life and death struggle. Exacerbating the diabolical nature of the violent life and death drama professionally referred to as "Victim Precipitated Homicide," more commonly referred to, as "Suicide by Cop," was the fact that all involved – perpetrator and police – were members of the same fraternity known as the New York State Police.

The sudden explosion of a weapon, fired by one of the officer's would free Lenny of the demons that tortured him; however, the pulling of that trigger also ended Lenny's life.

Lenny's tragic demise troubled me greatly because during my tenure in the state police, he had become like a son to me. I was one of the few people able to penetrate the barriers he threw up during his bouts of depression. How I wish that on that fateful fall evening I could have been called upon to quench the firestorm of emotion that drove Lenny toward personal destruction.

Lenny Kasson was a hero in life, and will remain a hero in death. It is a certainty that his soul is now at peace.

Leonard C. Kasson

About the Author

A native of Cortland, New York, Wayne E. Beyea served a 25 year career in the New York State Police as Trooper, Investigator and Senior Investigator, supervising a Bureau of Criminal Investigation Unit (BCI) in the Hudson Valley for 9 years.

He is a graduate of Ulster Community College, Stone Ridge, New York, attaining a degree in Criminal Justice.

Specially trained as a hostage negotiator by the New York State Police, New York City Police and Federal Bureau of Investigation, he successfully negotiated several hostage incidents, which led to his assignment as Coordinator of the New York State Police Hostage Negotiation Training Program. While coordinator, he supervised numerous hostage negotiations, talked barricaded felons into surrender, prevented many suicides and in one bizarre incident, was nearly shot by a police supervisor.

After retirement from law enforcement he began writing and has had numerous short stories published in a weekly publication. He was hired as a writer by "Strictly Business" a monthly, North Country, glossy magazine, and worked for the publication, until accepting employment with Clinton County to institute a Restorative Justice Program dealing with juvenile crime.

In retirement Wayne has authored his autobiography, *Reflections From the Shield,* and *Fatal Impeachment,* a crime fiction, both published by IUniverse.

A Day Off From the Farm:
A U.S. Marine in Vietnam

By Zach Foster

Victor E. Jonas, Commander of DAV Joe Gibbs Chapter 44—my personal friend and mentor—was born in 1944 on his family's farm in Muscoda, Wisconsin. The Jonas family, of German-Bohemian descent, had a 500 acre dairy farm with a lake and made their living on the farm. As a child, Vic attended a one-room grade school with fifteen students, ranging from the First to Eighth Grades. School was a wonderful time of day for him, since it would give him a few hours away from working sun-up to sun-down on the farm.

Living in the countryside, the Jonas family would often go hunting. Vic received his first rifle at the age of ten and has hunted ever since.

After graduating from the eighth grade, Vic went on to attend the local high school, playing all the sports in the school and becoming a letterman. At the age of seventeen Vic, still a senior in high school, enlisted in the inactive Marine Corps Reserve. This was a decision his parents were initially wary of. No one in the family had served in the military since the 1800's. His maternal great grandfather had ridden in the cavalry with George Custer, and his paternal great grandfather fought in the Civil War for the U.S., surviving wounds sustained at Thatcher's Run in 1865. Vic's Parents were also concerned with the time that the Marine Corps would take Vic away from farm labor. In the end, though, they supported their son's decision to enlist.

Vic's reserve status was a delayed entry program, in which he was allowed to finish high school after his enlistment. Also, the inactive time between his enlistment and basic training counted as Reserve time before he entered Active Duty. After his initial enlistment, he was taken from rural Wisconsin to Des Moines, Iowa for medical examinations. He almost didn't get in due to a heart murmur, but since he'd played football for several years without health problems, he was allowed to get into the Corps.

That summer he went to Basic Combat Training at MCRD San Diego. He recalls that his feet went flat from running during boot camp, but he persevered. At the end of boot camp he was given the option of a medical discharge for his flat feet, but he chose to remain in the Corps. While many current and former Marines remember the hellish trials of boot camp, Vic fondly remembers it as a wonderful day off from the farm.

After graduating from Basic, Vic went on to AIT at Camp Pendleton. Weapons qualification was easy for him, having consistently shot rifles since the age of ten, and he quickly broke the range record with the M14. It was during AIT that Vic started to become aware of the harsh life of Marines during the draft era. Many convicts were given the choice of prison or military, and a great many of them entered the Corps, bringing their hostile attitudes with them.

The first time he really tried to kill a man was during AIT. Vic was ill with the flu, which excused no Marine from training, and his platoon was running up a mountain called Little Agony, carrying a pack and rifle. The squad leader behind Vic would hit him in the lower back with the metal-plated butt of his M14 every time he would start to lag. After being hit the fourth time, each stroke having caused him massive pain, Vic turned to the man and threatened, "You hit me again, I'll kill your ass!"

The squad leader struck him a fifth time in the lower back, and without hesitation Vic spun around with his rifle and hit the squad leader in the chin with the rifle butt, causing a piece of his jaw to fly out of his mouth. This almost caused a race riot within the platoon, since Vic was white and the squad leader was black, and immediately the other black men began to fit their bayonets and shout threats to Vic. Though the military had been integrated for over a decade, racial tensions were still high in the 1960's.

The drill instructors broke up the hostilities and took Vic to the dispensary for the Provost Marshall to deal with. Vic could have been sentenced to life in prison at Fort Leavenworth, but he was acquitted of all charges. After a medical examination, it was revealed that Vic had suffered two broken vertebrae from being struck in the back, and one more hit could have paralyzed or killed him. He rejoined his platoon, with MP's guarding him until the tensions died down.

There was another instance at AIT where violence flared. The Marines were in line one morning to get chow and people were getting rowdy. Two Marines suddenly got into a brutal fist fight, and one got the other against the wall where he pounded the man to death.

Vic was glad to finally complete AIT. He was sent to El Toro base for fourteen weeks to be trained on driving every vehicle in the Marine Corps. He was then transferred out to be with the Third Marine Division at 29 Palms, California. The Third Marines went on a troop ship to Hawaii, Korea, mainland Japan, and then to Okinawa, where they'd be stationed for the next eighteen months.

During this time Vic would see no promotions, as a Marine could serve for over a decade before making Corporal. He was stationed at Camp Sucran for three months working as a truck driver.

One thing every service member stationed on Okinawa found out was that there was a huge rivalry between the Third Marines and the Army's 173rd Airborne Division. Fist fights broke out all the time. However, it was a fist fight with a fellow Marine that landed Vic with disciplinary action.

He and the Marine were drunk after a night of partying and they got a cab ride home together. In their intoxication they managed to get into a fist fight and both were quickly run up for disciplinary action. The man with the gavel was a Major Batey, who told Vic, "Jonas, you like to fight. Hell, you've got a rep! Because I'm a nice guy I'm going to give you a choice: six months in the brig, or you can volunteer at this moment to join the boxing team."

Vic left that office having got off scot-free as the newest boxer on Okinawa. There was a lot of prestige in being a boxer, but the downside was that boxers never got liberty, and Vic had to stomach a drink of twelve raw eggs every morning, along with eating several oranges. Each day the boxers would pump iron, run long distances, and practice fighting.

Vic fought three official matches and won all three. The first two were victories by knockout, but the third was a win by scoring points. Though he won that third match, Vic took a lot of nasty hits to the head and body and it didn't take him long to decide that he hated being a boxer more than anything in the world. It was still a day off from the farm back in Wisconsin, though.

After the match, Vic marched into Major Batey's office and said, "Sir, you can go ahead and send me to the brig, I don't care. I just ain't boxing anymore."

Major Batey looked at him, smiled, and said "Jonas, get the hell out of my office." Vic left, having quit the boxing team, and he realized he'd been had; Major Batey was never going to send him to the brig, he just needed a fighter for the time being.

The year 1965 came and tensions in Southeast Asia were at their peak. The Marine Corps was preparing to deploy combat troops to Vietnam. The Third Marines were all receiving their inoculations, and Vic was one of the thousands of young men in line to receive a series of shots.

After getting all the painful vaccinations, Vic was told to go down to his rack and wait for further instruction. This was one of the few instances where Vic didn't know what he was in trouble for. As he was later told, Vic had gone over two years on Active Duty without leave, and was forced to go back to Wisconsin for overdue leave.

This is how Vic just missed the historic landing at Da Nang. When his leave was over, he went back to Okinawa to prepare to deploy for Vietnam, but he was presented with other factors that would delay his deployment. First, because he was ordered to go on mandatory leave before he'd received his vaccinations, there was no record that he did indeed get his shots, so he had to be inoculated all over again.

However, he did receive an offer to transfer into the First Marines, which would have sped up his deployment to Vietnam. If he accepted the transfer, he would have been instantly promoted to Corporal. Needless to say, Vic jumped at the offer, since he was anxious to join the fighting in Vietnam and he would receive a hard to come by promotion with its corresponding pay raise. Though he was being promoted, it was much to his dissatisfaction that the Corps sweetened the deal by granting him thirty extra days of leave, which he had no choice but to take.

Vic recalls that "it was LBJ's war then. He was sending all kinds of convoys to Southeast Asia—it was the biggest convoy since World War II." Vic at last got his place aboard one of the ships in these convoys. There was a point 40 miles off shore from Vietnam that a typhoon hit and sank two STI ships. The troop transports swayed heavily, and Vic recalls that rivers of vomit ran three inches deep.

Finally arriving at Chu Lai, Vic was stationed at the First Marines' headquarters to join Operation Utah. The base had a perimeter set up near Highway 1, with a battery of 155 M109 self-propelled Howitzer cannons just south of Chu Lai. The Howitzers were lined up along a ridge overlooking the valley. There was another hillside close by from which the Viet Cong enjoyed harassing the Marines.

Vic vividly remembers his first taste of combat. It was a day in early 1966 when an unknown number of

Vietcong and North Vietnamese regulars attempted to overrun the perimeter near Chu Lai. The Howitzers began firing to kill as many enemy troops as possible. The guns initially were firing at a forty-five degree angle but soon were firing at point blank range as the NVA and VC worked their way to the perimeter, throwing heavy harassing fire at the Marines' front.

The hill the Howitzers were positioned on and the hill the Communist troops were coming from were separated by a ravine. The Marines had a strong defense there behind the Howitzers. While most of the Infantrymen had good cover behind trees or sandbags, Vic was one of two Marines firing from a ditch dug into the Marines' side of the ravine, out in the danger zone. He was "scared as shit," and wondered what he had gotten himself into and whether or not he would live until dawn. For two nights the enemy troops continuously sent squads of five to six men to shoot at the guns and the Marines. They occasionally sent squads during the day.

At one point Vic went behind the Howitzers on an ammo run during a short lull in the fighting. On his way back he was knocked down by a muzzle blast when the Howitzer crew accidentally fired a round. The blast blew out his eardrum, but he didn't have time to worry about it as he continued to prepare for the next wave of enemy troops.

The firefight ended on the third day, with 125 Marines dead and over 1,200 NVA and VC dead. The Marines counted the enemy dead, some of them returning with memorabilia. Vic only got an old web belt and a "kitchen knife."

After the battle Vic and his company were sent back to Chu Lai for some rest, but then were sent out almost immediately following their return to base. Vic was assigned to a tank retriever crew as their new .50 cal gunner. Of course, any Marine operating any kind of big gun could almost guarantee being shot at.

After the Communist forces failed to overrun the Marines around Chu Lai, the Viet Cong began to routinely harass them with 80 mm mortar shells and small arms fire. It was upon surviving his first mortar attack that the war changed for Vic—he got over his big fear of dying. Sure, he certainly didn't want it and he would do everything possible to avoid dying, but it somehow lost it stigma; its edge.

It finally occurred to him that he was most likely going to die. Too many guys were getting killed left and right and he still had his whole tour of duty to go. To make the odds worse, he and every Marine in his unit received a piece of paper from the Navy Department stating that until further notice, they were indefinitely in the Marine Corps. From then on he would hang up his fears and worries, knowing that the end was always just around the corner. To this day he says about war, "It's a game of cards and you never know when they'll take all, so you might as well take out as many of 'em as possible."

As several hundred Marines were killed in the coming weeks, rank slots opened up and Vic was promoted to E5, Sergeant. After his promotion he was given a top secret in-country clearance. He reported to the Intelligence tent where he would be receiving his assignments. His new Officer-In-Charge introduced him to a Master Sergeant (name withheld), a lifer and hardened veteran of the Korean War.

Vic would be leading search and destroy missions, and training was quick. The Master Sergeant took a squad consisting of Vic and five others to seek and kill enemy troops to show them the ropes. He took them out twice, and after that Vic led the ambushes.

Sometimes they would make hard contact with the Viet Cong, and other times they would find nothing. The one thing that particularly bothered Vic was that they weren't allowed to wear helmets for fear that something might clang on them and jeopardize their position. For this they went to combat wearing soft covers.

After a search and destroy mission, Vic would be granted one day's rest and then the following day would be assigned to work base security. Then he would either drive tank retrievers for the motor pool or work base security until the next ambush. He would often see the Master Sergeant from Intelligence around the base. Vic recalls amusedly that the Master Sergeant had a metal plate in his head and it drove the man nuts whenever it rained.

It wasn't long before Vic was wounded. It was a day out in the bush when his company was setting up defensive positions, waiting for the almost guaranteed nightly Viet Cong push. Vic was performing his duties as a sergeant by making sure that his men were properly dug in and with ample protection. One Lance Corporal, a man named Manbeck, only had one row of sandbags in front of his foxhole. Vic told him to make a second row, to which Manbeck grumbled, and then Vic loudly ordered him to do so. He did.

Shortly after, Vic was walking in front of the foxholes, making sure they were all acceptable to fight from, when the nearby tree line opened up with bullets flying at the Marines. Vic dove into a foxhole and on the way down he felt as if a mule had kicked him square in the head.

The machine gunner told him, "Sergeant, you're hit!" Vic was obviously still breathing, so he wasted no time feeding ammunition to the machine gunner. A bullet had scraped his forehead during the fall, which would have killed Vic had he only been one inch lower.

The fight lasted twenty minutes, with the machine gunner pelting the VC and the VC retreating into the jungle as they usually did, dragging their dead along with them. After the fight, Manbeck saw that his layers of sandbags, which were increased upon Vic's order, had been whittled down by bullets to a few rags and some spilled sand. He immediately jumped up and hugged

Vic, saying "Thank you Sergeant Jonas! Thank you! I'll listen to you now! Thank you Sergeant!"

Manbeck was Jewish, and as a celebration of his life being saved by his Sergeant's vigilance, he ate pork with the other Marines. Vic's wound was a graze, not deep, and he was alright. He would be wounded two more times in Vietnam. When asked why he never had the medic put him in for a Purple Heart medal, Vic said, "When the shit's flying, the last thing you're worried about is getting a ribbon pinned on your ass."

For every soldier serving a war, despite the overall hardship, there are some definitively good times that will never be forgotten, such as having fun drinking with platoon mates, firefights where the whole team makes it out alive, the forging of good friendships and the ability to care for friends despite the hostile environment. There are also unspeakable horrors that will never be forgotten, such as the loss of many good friends in a short time.

There was a mission in which the Marines set up a temporary perimeter north of Chu Lai, near a village inhabited by an estimated 200 people where the joint forces had been spraying Agent Orange to clear brush for guns. Their position had ten to twelve-foot high concertina wire, machine gun placement, and a perimeter established.

The village was very close by, with a few hundred yards of trees and brush separating the Marines from a suspected Viet Cong base of local operations. There was also a dirt road that led to the perimeter and through the camp. At this gate were two machine gun nests. Around the perimeter the guards would patrol with their M14 rifles.

The locals were no friends to the Americans, and the Marines' suspicions of hostile locals were proven correct. At night sometimes the villagers, probably the local Viet Cong, would swing lanterns through the trees, chanting "GI you die." The Viet Cong did a good job not being seen unless they intended to be seen.

Vic's squad was on the perimeter one night when a twelve man VC death squad attacked the Marines. The only thing visible in the thick darkness was the road and what looked to be silhouettes. For some reason there was a failure in planning the guard stations, and there was no one manning the machine gun nests on the road.

As soon as the Viet Cong figured out that the machine guns were unmanned, they ran to the base camp. They seemed to make it inside the perimeter in a heartbeat. Vic saw them running in and, shooting on full automatic, sprayed the area where they were. After five seconds of shooting and yelling everywhere, things started blowing up all over the camp as the suicide squad scattered in every direction. They had grenades, satchel charges, and AK-47 rifles.

One of them ran to where there were tents near an electrical generator and some lights. Vic had a good friend there, a tall, 250-pound black Sergeant who was making his way out of his tent amidst the confusion. Vic witnessed in horror as the VC ran behind the tent and threw a grenade in there. The grenade exploded and his friend's legs were gone.

The VC tried to escape the tent area and ran towards Vic's squad, not knowing they were there. The VC was shot down quickly, and then Vic and his squad went to help the wounded, with Vic heading straight to his friend.

The assault was over quite quickly, every Viet Cong having caused massive damage before being killed. The chopper crews wasted no time loading up the wounded to be evacuated. Vic picked up his friend, now half-sized, and took him to a chopper. The gunner on the chopper said, "Put him aside, Sergeant, he's dead."

"He ain't dead," Vic told him, "you save him!"

Not in a mood to argue, the gunner let the body go on. Then the chopper took off for about twenty feet, landed, and the body was rolled off. Someone else took the Corporal and wrapped him in a poncho, and took him where the other dead and wounded were.

After the ordeal was over Vic picked up the dead VC and threw his body onto the concertina wire, were it was caught hanging eight feet up. He fired some shots into it, and left it for the night.

Time passed and there was another mission that the First Marines, including Vic's unit, were sent on. They were situated on defensive positions on a hill south of

Chu Lai. The hill was surrounded by a large grassy valley. At the top of the hill was a tank, and the on the rest of the hill were foxholes on all sides. The North Vietnamese regular army was making a big push to Chu Lai and it was the Marines' job to keep them off the hill. They were armed only with their rifles, a few hand grenades, and the .50 cal gun on the tank.

Evening came and it was another mundane night for Vic, who was sitting in a foxhole with another Sergeant, Jerry Pennington, chatting, enduring the heat and swatting mosquitoes. It was 10 P.M. and looking down into the valley, Vic noticed that the elephant grass seemed to be swaying, moving like seismic waves.

"Jerry," Vic said, "the fucking grass is moving. There ain't no wind!" A chopper was flying over the valley and dropped flares. All at once the back side of the hill was illuminated by a solid wall of tracer bullets going uphill. A terrific firefight ensued as the NVA charged up the other side of the hill, with more trying to charge up the side where Vic's squad was.

At the top of the hill the tank's .50 caliber gun was firing down at the swarms of NVA troops, killing many of them until it suddenly stopped firing. The NVA had made their way up the backside of the hill, killing every Marine on the way up, and they killed the tank crew as they took control of the hilltop.

They then mounted the .50 cal and fired one round down hill at the remaining Marines. The bullet flew right between Vic and Jerry. Every Marine that was still left immediately fired in whichever direction an NVA troop could be seen. At that point in time, the point Sergeant, a man named Hill, took his squad and charged up the hill to retake it from the NVA. Hill's squad soon took the top of the hill, and then the NVA started retreating down hill on all sides. Vic's squad fired continuously at them as they came down at them, with one squad member firing downhill, shooting them in the back.

As the Marines desperately fought to stay alive, air support came over the valley and fires at the waves of enemy troops. The famous chopper gunship "Puff the Magic Dragon" came five or six times that night with rockets and chain guns, pelting anything that moved.

Morning came and the battle was finally over, the NVA having finally retreated. While Marines counted the dead, Vic had his squad pile several dozen enemy bodies. There was something very particular about these North Vietnamese soldiers. Many of these corpses were at least six feet tall, and more pale-skinned than any of the Vietnamese they'd dealt with before.

As the body counts were being taken, the unit commander flew from HQ and his chopper landed on top of the hill. Vic asked to speak to him and pointed the pile of bodies out to the commander.

"Sir," Vic said to him, "we're killing Chinese here."

"What are you saying, Sergeant?" the Colonel asked sternly.

"Sir," Vic continued, "these dinks are way too big to be North Vietnamese regulars."

The Colonel, looking like he might know something, said sternly and harshly to Vic, "Sergeant, I won't tell you how to do your job and you won't tell me how to run my war! Keep your mouth shut! Is that understood?"

Vic and his squad caught a truck ride back to Chu Lai. As they got on the trucks, choppers came down looking for a landing zone. There were so many enemy corpses on and around the hill, they couldn't land without crushing dead bodies.

The official body count was somewhere near one thousand, though the Marines had no doubt that the Communist troops dragged off at least several hundred of their own dead. Vic estimates that they killed from two to two and a half thousand North Vietnamese "regulars."

After the big push, things went back to normal around Chu Lai. Vic continued to do his regular duties of driving tank retrievers, doing base security, and leading many ambushes out in the bush. After a while, Vic became combat weary and figured out that he was being sent out to combat more often that was his turn.

He requested to speak to his Officer In Charge, and eventually he was brought to the officer's tent. Vic explained his grievance that constantly being sent on ambushes out of turn was going to get him killed.

The officer said, "Sergeant, you are absolutely right. I do send you out on as many ambushes as possible. The truth of the matter is that you're a good leader; you bring my Marines back alive and in one piece. Other guys go out on ambushes and then get some eighteen-year-old kid killed and then I have to write to his grieving parents about what a great Marine he was. But you, Sergeant, you bring back my Marines. I do send you out on ambushes often and I will continue to send you out on ambushes, because you are damn good at it. Are we understood?"

"Yes sir. Thank you, sir."

Towards the end of his tour Vic had filled out some paperwork to get enrolled into college. His unit was out in the bush one night when a runner came to his foxhole and said, "Sergeant Jonas, you're going home." He was getting out on a college discharge.

Vic was taken back to headquarters at Chu Lai where he turned in all his equipment. He was nearly in tears when they took away his rifle, since it had been his lifeline for the past year. Now, it was at the armory. Vic left Vietnam, having earned two Bronze Stars with a V for Valor, and was sent to Okinawa until his discharge went through.

By 1967 Vietnam was long behind him and Vic was attending the University of Wisconsin at Platteville. Student life was difficult for Vic. Even though he was out of Vietnam and moving on with his life, anti-war demonstrations were breaking out all over campus. As soon as the protestors found out he was a Vietnam Veteran, they would constantly harass Vic, often antagonizing him into fist fights. Soon, the school administrators wouldn't allow Vic to live on the main campus because of the agitation between him and the draft dodgers. This man who had fought hard and kept so many of his fellow Marines alive was reduced by ignorant civilians to living on the school's farm in a converted chicken coop.

Vic was having a beer at the local bar one afternoon when a man in his forties dressed in a sharp suit came and drank a beer next to him. "How're you doing, Sergeant? Good old America isn't what you thought it would be, is it?"

"No, it sucks," Vic replied, not knowing who this man was, but having a good idea that he was from the Department of Defense.

The man was from the CIA. The CIA had heard of what a great shot Vic had been in the Marine Corps and this man had been sent to recruit him. "How would you like to make some good money?" that man asked. He was trying to get Vic do to a special assignment.

Vic was offered to be a sniper for the CIA, guarding oil lines in Saudi Arabia. He would be paid $20,000 just for agreeing to do it. He would be paid another $20,000 for being a CIA shooter for six months. Then he would be paid an additional $20,000 for completing his six months for the CIA. After the six months, he would go back in the Marine Corps as an E7 Gunnery Sergeant—two rank promotions above Sergeant.

It sounded like a sweet deal to Vic. He thought it over for a moment and told the man, "I ain't never killed anyone for money, and I ain't gonna start." He was a man whose days off from the family farm were honorable devoted to serving his country in a war. He had done his time, and he was tired of killing.

After one year and one summer school at the University of Wisconsin, Vic left the school. He decided that if there was a life for him, it wasn't in rural Wisconsin. On a warm, sunny day he stepped out onto the traveler's road and hitched a ride to California with $300 in his pocket.

A Day Off From the Farm:
A U.S. Marine in Vietnam

About the Author

Zach Foster was born and raised in southern California, where he lives with his family. He earned the Eagle Scout award in 2007 and soon after enlisted in the California State Military Reserve, where he currently serves as a Specialist (E4). He deeply enjoys writing fiction stories and non-fiction essays. He is working towards a degree in Political Science and one day hopes to run for public office.